Also available by Martyn Waites

For more information visit www.martynwaites.com
and www.taniacarver.com and follow Martyn Waites on
Twitter @MartynWaites

ANGEL OF DEATH

Originally published in 1983, Susan Hill's *The Woman in Black* has sold over half a million copies in the UK alone. As a play, it's been showing to packed theatres around the world since 1989, and is currently the second longest-running play in the history of the West End, after *The Mousetrap*.

The film was released in 2012. Starring Daniel Radcliffe, it became the highest-grossing UK horror film of all time. Its sequel, *The Woman in Black: Angel of Death*, is scheduled for major release on the big screen in 2014.

THE
WOMAN IN BLACK

ANGEL OF DEATH

Martyn Waites

Published by Arrow Books 2014

2 4 6 8 10 9 7 5 3 1

Copyright © Martyn Waites 2013

Based on an original idea by Susan Hill and an original script by Jon Croker

Martyn Waites has asserted his right under the Copyright, Designs
and Patents Act 1988 to be identified as the author of this work.

This novel is a work of fiction. Apart from references to actual figures and places,
all other names and characters are a product of the author's imagination and any
resemblance to real persons, living or dead, is purely coincidental.

First published in Great Britain in 2013 by
Arrow Books in association with Hammer
Random House, 20 Vauxhall Bridge Road,
London SW1V 2SA

www.randomhouse.co.uk
www.hammerfilms.com

Addresses for companies within The Random House Group Limited can
be found at: www.randomhouse.co.uk/offices.htm

The Random House Group Limited Reg. No. 954009

A CIP catalogue record for this book
is available from the British Library

ISBN 9780099588290

The Random House Group Limited supports the Forest Stewardship
Council® (FSC®), the leading international forest-certification organisation.
Our books carrying the FSC label are printed on FSC®-certified paper. FSC
is the only forest-certification scheme supported by the leading environmental
organisations, including Greenpeace. Our paper procurement policy can
be found at: www.randomhouse.co.uk/environment

Typeset in Centaur MT by SX Composing DTP, Rayleigh, Essex, SS6 7XF
Printed and bound by CPI Group (UK) Ltd, Croydon, CR0 4YY

The House

Eel Marsh House. Dank, dilapidated, unloved and unlived in.

It has stood alone on Eel Marsh Island for the best part of a century. Surrounded by swirling, damp mist that paints it darker and greyer, and by clammy, cold drizzle that renders it indistinct, it looms out of the fog. Empty. But not silent.

The water swirls and susurrates around the island the house has been built on. It laps the edges of the marsh that surrounds it. It permeates through the softer ground, turning it to quicksand, ready to claim the lives of travellers who have strayed, pull them under and close above them once more, swallow them whole, leave the surface undisturbed, as if no one has ever been there. Beneath the surface, the water churns with the eels' constant slithering and writhing; snakes with angry faces, they feed on whatever living matter makes its way down to them.

The house has been undisturbed for decades. An ancient pile of heavy stone, it has weathered but endured, crumbling but still upright. But there is movement on the island, in the house. Recent. Unwelcome.

The front door is pushed open. It throws light on darkness, causes dust to rise, small animals to scurry for the shadows. Paintings have been taken from walls, old photographs, documents, papers, ornaments have all been thrown in boxes, stored away.

In their place different things come into the house. Unfamiliar things. Alien things. Heavy, black curtains have been put up at the windows, creating a new world within. Wrought-iron beds have been carried up the stairs, arranged in the bedrooms and mattresses placed on top. The house is to have new occupants.

Now, thick black cable snakes through the house, taking on twisted, serpentine shapes, a dark mirror of the eels writhing in the water below and around it. The one cable connects to a generator that casts a hum down the halls and through the rooms. Gas masks hang from hooks, their blank, round-eyed stares the first welcome newcomers will receive.

The overgrown grounds outside the house have also been cleared. Slowly, a garden, long since subsumed by wilderness, is beginning to emerge. And with it the rest of the island. Even *the stones in the graveyard have had ivy and moss cleared from them, making their names legible once more.*

The house is ready.

The house is waiting.

The Boy

The British Spitfire banked high then turned, and, engines screeching, swooped down low over the platoon of soldiers, its two front-mounted machine guns belching rapid-fire death.

The soldiers screamed, '*Achtung! Schnell! Heil Hitler!*' They were dressed in the khaki uniforms of English infantrymen, but they spoke with German comic-strip voices. They fell on to their backs and sides, lying heavy and unmoving, legs in the air, arms still holding rifles, still raised.

The Spitfire banked upwards once more and came round again, screaming as it did so. The pilot spoke into his communicator in smooth, calm RAF tones, his valedictory speech overlaid by static. The plane was poised, ready to swoop down again, to kill the few German soldiers who remained standing. The throttle was open, the screaming of the engines increased—

The plane stopped. Completely still. It hovered in mid-air.

The boy holding it put his head up, cocked on one side, listening.

He had heard something. A voice. Calling for him. And only him.

He turned and walked towards the window, drawn to the voice. His game forgotten, he was oblivious to the tin soldiers on the floor. His feet came down, crushing them, snapping them, bending them out of shape.

He was playing in an upstairs room of what was left of a bomb-damaged house. His own house was on the other side of the street, the only street in the area still left standing. All the rest had been demolished by German bombs.

The voice was insistent, drawing him on. He reached the window, stopped before the broken glass. He leaned forward, pushing his head slowly through the empty square, his neck close to the razored edges.

A dark silhouette of a woman stood in a doorway on the opposite side of the street.

'Edward! Edward!'

It was His mother.

'Get here, now. Quick . . .'

The boy blinked behind his thick glasses. He could hear the noise of a plane, not the plane from his previous game, but a real one. He listened again. A whole squadron of planes approaching, and, above that, the depressingly familiar whine of the air-raid siren.

He looked down at the doorway once more. His mother was gesturing to him, telling him to hurry, get out of the building, get down to the shelter. She was dressed in her black wool coat, her weddings and funerals and church coat, the one she always wore in an air raid.

'My only good coat,' he had heard her say often. 'They'll have to bury me in this.'

The boy looked at the toy plane, still in his hand, then up at the sky. Real planes were approaching, none of them Spitfires. He let the plane fall to the floor, and a small cloud of dust rose from the bare floorboards as it landed. He turned away from the window, anxious now, ready to run downstairs.

Time stopped, held its breath, then sped up, and the boy heard the end of the world in his head as he was thrown backwards across the shaking floor, the remaining glass in the windows shattering, flying after him.

When Edward opened his eyes he thought he must be in Heaven.

He blinked. Sat up. No. He was still in the upstairs room, still where he had fallen. He checked himself over, found that he could still move. His body hurt, but he didn't seem to have broken anything. He let out a small, rough laugh. He was alive. He had survived.

His face was itchy and wet, stinging. He rubbed it. It felt like sandpaper, rough and sore. He took his hand away, studied it. Blood. He had been cut by flying glass.

He ran over to what was left of the window, ready to call out, to give his mother the good news, tell her not to worry.

But his mother wasn't there.

There was just a pile of rubble where the house had been, out of which was poking the hem of a black coat.

Edward stared, unable to move, as he began to understand what had happened. Tears formed in his eyes, started to roll down his cheeks, mixing with the blood.

His mother was gone. Dead.

Grief welled up inside him then, bubbling, dark and toxic. He screamed and sobbed and screamed some more, screaming his pain at the world as if he would never stop.

Hope in Their Eyes

Eve Parkins knew there were worse things to fear than the dark. But that didn't mean she enjoyed it. Or that she ever would.

The Tube station was becoming more familiar to her than her own bedroom. It had been the same routine for over a month now. Lying shivering on the platform, night after night, wrapped up in blankets and huddled next to complete strangers on the flagged floor and against the cold porcelain wall tiles, like shrouded, slabbed corpses in a mortuary. Each one of them praying that tonight would be the night that the Luftwaffe would miss, that the anti-aircraft guns would get lucky, that the RAF had managed some daytime bombing of their own over the Channel to deplete the German numbers.

That no one would die, at least not any of them. That there would still be a city left for them in the morning.

She looked along the row of people. All of life was here, she thought, on the platform with her. Young, old, fat, thin, and everything in between. All different, yet all the same, their faces displaying the same tiredness, the same desolation.

Some were attempting to sing. A few choruses of 'The White Cliffs of Dover' to keep morale up. After the first chorus most of the voices petered out.

'I'll never forget the people I met . . .'

A lone voice sang on, wavering, echoing round the cold walls and away down the tunnel.

'Braving those angry skies . . .'

Others joined in once more, their voices stirring, trying to rise. But it still sounded hollow, haunted.

'I remember well as the shadows fell, the light of hope in their eyes . . .'

The voices died away. No one moved.

The drone of engines could be heard from outside, from above. Everyone knew what that meant. The staccato bursts of anti-aircraft fire that answered the drone just confirmed it.

The bombers were back.

There was another whine, different to the engine drone. Then another. And another.

Everyone held their breath. The oil lamps strung along the walls illuminated trembling bodies, fearful eyes.

Then the bombs hit. The walls shuddered and shivered. Plaster and dust fell. People flinched, jumped. A few let out moans and screams, then tried to regain control of themselves. It didn't do to break down in front of others.

Eve closed her eyes, tried to take herself somewhere else, somewhere warm and sunny and safe.

Another explosion. Another drizzle of dust and plaster.

Eve opened her eyes once more. It was no good. She was here. Now. The bombs wouldn't go away by wishing them to, so she just had to deal with the situation.

She looked across the row of faces, her gaze settling on a little boy. He was dressed in his pyjamas, his hair sticking out at all angles. In his hands he clutched a threadbare teddy, clinging to it like his life depended on it. With every distant explosion his eyes darted about in terror, another tear threatening to fall from them.

Eve felt something inside her break and moved to sit beside him. She smiled. It was a warm smile and it illuminated her face, giving it a certain radiance, even in the oil-lit darkness.

'What's his name?' she asked, looking down at the teddy.

The boy stared at her, barely able to speak. 'Bear,' he said eventually, his voice as small and threadbare as his toy.

'And are you looking after him?'

The boy nodded.

'So will you make sure he doesn't get scared?'

The boy thought for a moment, looked at his bear, then back at Eve. He nodded again.

'That's good,' said Eve. 'We need brave boys like you.'

Her smile deepened, fixed on him, and the boy gradually smiled back. Safe now, reassured.

'How do you do it?'

A woman was huddled against the wall in a blanket alongside her. She was older than Eve, only by a few years, but the worry and exhaustion in her features made her seem even older still. Eve turned towards her, frowning slightly.

'Night after night of this,' said the woman, 'and you're still smiling . . .'

Before answering, Eve glanced down the tunnel once more. It was dark, empty, seemingly endless.

'You've got to, haven't you?' she said, her voice as cheerful as she could make it.

The woman didn't seem so sure. It looked like the fatigue and strain would get her before the bombs did. She frowned at Eve, clearly not believing her words.

Under the woman's gaze, Eve's smile faltered and she looked away, down into the tunnel once more.

The next morning was dull and grey, depressing and wintery, as Eve emerged from the Tube station brushing the dust from her clothes. She had survived another night.

She looked round. The city was even more shattered and scarred than the night before. The bombed-out remains of shops, pubs and houses were everywhere. A broken mannequin dangled from a shattered shop window, swaying like a hanged looter. All that remained of the floor above was a wall with an intact fireplace, but no floor, no hearth. Next to it was a cupboard, the door creaking in the breeze, a stack of Cornishware bowls teeter-tottering on the shelf. They fell, smashing, adding to the rubble. Someone's family photographs blew down the street; smiling, happy children borne away, memories, markers of a life, lost for ever.

Eve was alive. But the city seemed dead.

She checked her watch as she hurried home. She had to pack. She was leaving.

Safer in the Country

Eve was only slightly out of breath as, smartly dressed and suitcase in hand, she walked into King's Cross station. She needed to make a fresh start, she thought. And today would be the day to do it. She was leaving the city. Going somewhere safe.

Soot covered the ceiling glass inside the station, as steam from the trains drifted above their heads. The place was alive with comings and goings, the clang and clatter of the trains and the passengers. Joyful reunions and tearful goodbyes were all around her. The air was filled with a frantic, nervous energy as hope and despair turned routine departures and arrivals into matters of life and death.

Posters covered all the walls of the station. Several variations of 'Careless Talk Costs Lives' were dotted about, as were invocations to 'Dig for Victory'. A stern, red-faced and angry-looking man dressed in full John Bull regalia standing in front of a line of infantrymen pointed an accusing finger at all who walked past, and asked, 'WHO'S ABSENT? Is it YOU?'

The poster made Eve notice the soldiers all the more. The young, fresh-faced, optimistic ones, eager to engage the Hun in battle, contrasted with the wounded, broken men who were returning. Heads were turned, eyes downcast as they made their way through the concourse. The young soldiers making a point of not looking at the returnees, ignoring them in case their bad luck turned into an airborne infection.

She heard sobbing just behind her and, turning, saw a mother with her daughter. It was difficult to make out who was crying the most. The mother clung on to her daughter, and the daughter did the same until well-meaning relatives separated them both, taking the girl away. 'It's for her own good,' Eve heard. 'She'll be safer with us.' Eve thought of the boy in the Underground station the previous night. She hoped somebody was looking after him, making sure he was safe. The thought made her tearful.

'Mothers – send them out of London' said a poster on the wall above the sobbing mother. It showed a boy and girl in dressing gowns and pyjamas, against a brick wall. Huddled together, frightened and apprehensive, their eyes haunted and shell-shocked. Next to it another brother and sister, but these were bucolic, blonde, chubby cherubs. The boy, hair neatly parted and slicked down, held a protective arm round his kiss-curled little sister. They both looked contented and cheerful. Underneath was stated the reason for their happiness: 'CHILDREN are safer in the country . . . leave them there'.

Eve hoped so. Yes. She could only hope so.

It didn't take her long to find the woman she was meant to meet. A decade older than Eve, steel-eyed and ramrod-backed, standing as if to attention, Jean Hogg was Eve's headmistress.

Surrounding Jean was a group of children, all resembling the frightened children in the first poster. Jean had found something wrong with one of the boy's coats and was bending down to straighten it, admonishing him for not buttoning it properly, as Eve walked over to her.

'Good morning, Headmistress,' said Eve, smile in place. Then she looked at everyone else, giving them a bigger smile. 'Good morning, children.'

'Good morning, Miss Parkins.' They all spoke as one, the words said by rote in their usual sing-song voice. Some of them managed to return her smile. Eve felt a warmth inside her when they did that.

Jean straightened up, scrutinised her. For a second, Eve wondered whether the headmistress was going to find fault with her own coat.

'You're late,' said Jean.

'My . . . road was hit last night.'

Jean's expression suggested that a bomb was no excuse for unpunctuality, as Eve looked down at the children. There were seven of them, three girls and four boys, the youngest seven, the oldest eleven. They all had their own suitcase and each carried a small cardboard box with 'Gas Mask' written on the side. They were poor children, from the centre of the city, and none of them had their parents with them.

'Shall we find the train?' Eve asked.

'We're waiting for Edward.' From Jean's tone, Eve

could tell Edward had placed himself in an even worse category of tardiness than herself.

Eve frowned. 'I thought his mother was bringing him here.'

Jean's steely gaze — just for a second — gave way. 'Their house was hit two nights ago. He's an orphan now.' She looked away from Eve, eyes roving down the concourse. 'Here he is.'

Eve stared after her, still trying to take in what she had just heard. Edward — an orphan.

All the children had turned to watch Edward arrive, clamouring in their own way to be the first to see him. Eve knew what children were like. Anything out of the ordinary, different, was a source of spectacle, especially when it involved calamity and loss. Edward, whether he wanted to or not, would now be a celebrity.

Edward walked slowly towards the group, an older man holding his hand and leading him. But unlike the others he had no suitcase and was carrying all his belongings in a patched-up bag. The cuts on his face from the explosion had begun to heal and his glasses had been repaired, but Eve could tell from his expression how much he was hating being the centre of attention.

'Come on, Edward, there's a good chap,' said Jean, expecting her authority to carry automatically. 'We have a train to catch.'

She held out her hand to him, but Edward made no attempt to take it, or even move towards her. He clung on to the man at his side.

Eve moved quickly towards him, bending down so she was on his level. 'Edward,' she said, trying to get him to look at her, 'I'm so sorry . . .'

Edward didn't reply.

Eve tried a smile. 'You're . . . you're going to come away with us now,' she said. 'Away from all this.'

Edward still made no reply, and Eve eventually stood up.

'He hasn't said a word since the accident,' said the man. 'I take it you're his teacher?'

'Yes.'

'I'm just a neighbour. Been looking after him since . . . you know.' He gave the boy's hand a squeeze. 'Come on, Edward. Go with the nice lady. There's a good boy . . .'

The man let go of Edward. 'Don't forget your sweets,' he said, pushing a paper bag into Edward's pocket. Still Edward said nothing.

Eve took Edward's hand and looked into his

eyes once more. They were dulled, silent. There was nothing there. Nothing she could read.

Nothing she could reach.

She walked him over to the other children. It was time they were on the train and leaving London. Time for them to be safe once again.

Out of London

Even in the short space of time they had been on the train, Eve noticed the children's mood change. As the rubble of the bombed-out city gave way to smaller towns and finally countryside, the enormity of what was happening started to dawn on the children. They began to fidget in their seats, nervous with excitement. They were outside London, leaving their normal lives behind, off on an adventure into a new world.

Eve noticed that the children had divided themselves into two groups in the crowded carriage, boys and girls. Eve sat with the boys. Tom was the oldest and, if Eve was honest, the one she liked least. She knew it wasn't healthy for a teacher to think that way, not about children, but she couldn't help it. He had a pronounced mean streak that she had tried to cure him of, but to no avail. If there was any bullying to be done, Tom, she knew from experience, would be the one to do it.

Next to Tom was Alfie. Overweight and passionate about the RAF, he claimed he could identify a plane just by hearing its engines. But after the constant bombing raids on London, that wasn't a skill he was alone in possessing. Alfie and Tom were looking out of the window, fascinated by what they were seeing.

Opposite Tom and Alfie were James and Edward. James was Edward's best friend, but he clearly didn't know how to cope with the way Edward was now. He kept stealing glances at the mute, grief-stricken boy, his desire to help conflicting with his inability to do so written clearly on his features. Edward just stared at the bag of sweets in his lap.

Jean, her face hidden behind the *Daily Express*, was sitting with the three girls. The bossy Joyce; Ruby, her inseparable sidekick; and Flora. Flora's younger brother, Fraser, sniffing as if he had a permanent cold, was also sitting with them.

Flora was supposed to be keeping an eye on him, but she clearly wasn't doing so at the moment. Instead, she was staring at Edward. Eve knew that Flora had a little crush on Edward, but the way she was gazing at him now extended beyond that. Eve looked at the other children. They were all now staring at Edward, fascinated by his stillness, by the fact that he was simultaneously with them yet absent.

Jean lowered her newspaper. 'It's rude to stare, children.'

Joyce, Ruby, Flora and Fraser pointedly looked away from Edward and sat instead in awkward, wide-eyed silence.

'You may talk among yourselves,' said Jean, her voice slightly lower but still formal. 'Quietly.'

But they didn't. Not in front of Jean. Their headmistress was too imposing a figure for them to do that.

Eve took in the countryside rolling past the window, the colours Technicolor vivid after the drab monotones of London. Her eyes closed.

'You must have started young.'

She opened them again. The children were all still there, as was Jean, but someone else had joined them and had taken a seat opposite her in the crowded carriage.

He was young and handsome. They were the first things Eve noticed about him. He was also very smartly dressed. His RAF uniform showed the rank of captain.

'Excuse me?' she said.

He gestured towards the children. Eve couldn't help but notice the strength in his arm, the athleticism of the movement. 'To have eight children,' he said.

Eve smiled, felt herself redden slightly. 'They're not mine.'

The RAF captain returned her smile, raising an eyebrow. 'Kidnapped them, have you?'

'I'm their teacher.' Eve felt the carriage become suddenly warm.

'School trip?'

'Not exactly,' said Eve. 'Their parents can't leave London, and they've got no other relatives . . .' She shrugged. 'So we're taking them to a house in the country.'

The captain frowned. 'All by yourselves?'

'There's other schools going to be there, too.' Eve leaned forward, her face mock-serious. 'I don't know if you've heard, but there's a war on.'

The captain smiled again, about to respond, but Eve's attention had been diverted.

'Where did you get those?' She addressed Tom, the eldest boy, who was stuffing his face with liquorice root from a bag.

'James gave them to me,' Tom said, his mouth full.

Eve gave James a stern look. 'James, you know those are Edward's.'

'He wasn't eating them,' said James, but his voice lacked conviction.

Eve kept calm. Tom must have taken them and bullied James into taking the blame. She knew James was a decent boy, unlike Tom.

'Give them back and apologise,' she said.

'Yes, Miss,' said James. He took the bag of sweets from Tom and returned them to Edward. 'Sorry,' he said, looking Edward in the eyes.

But Edward made no sound. He didn't even move as the bag was placed in his lap.

'Where are you heading?'

It was the RAF captain again. His voice drew her away from the boys once more. She turned back to him. Put her smile in place.

'Am I being interrogated?'

He returned her smile. His eyes caught the light. 'Perhaps.'

Eve's smile deepened. 'Then I'd like to know your name and rank.'

'Captain Burstow,' he said, and Eve almost expected him to salute. 'But you can call me Harry.'

'Eve,' she said. 'But you can call me Miss Parkins.'

Harry did salute this time. 'Pleased to meet you, Miss Parkins. And may I ask where you're going?'

'You may,' she said. 'We're heading to Crythin Gifford.'

He raised his eyebrow once more, in genuine surprise this time. 'Really? Me too.'

'And what are you going to do there?'

'I'm a bomber pilot,' he said, trying to underplay the words, knowing it would impress her.

She gave a little laugh. 'That's what they all say.'

He shrugged. 'Somebody has to fly the planes.' His voice had changed, the tone darker, more serious.

Detecting an undertone of hurt to his words, Eve looked at him more closely. There was strength in his manner, and he had a stillness and calm that, to her, suggested a kind of defiance. But there had been something in his eyes. Just momentarily, when

27

he answered her; there, then gone. His defiance seemed to involve some kind of struggle within, rather than the war without. But she'd caught it, and recognised it.

He turned away from her, lit a cigarette.

'I'm . . . sorry,' said Eve. 'I didn't mean to . . .'

He looked back at her, smoke obscuring his features. 'It's top secret, so don't let anyone know.' He leaned forward, and the smoke dissipated. There was a glint in his eye. 'Otherwise I'll have to shoot you.'

'Don't worry,' said Eve, 'you can trust me.'

And she smiled at him once more. The smile that, she hoped, made everything all right.

Edward

Edward was frightened. He was on a station plat-form in the country, but nothing was familiar and he could see no one he knew.

Panic rose inside him. He was surrounded by adults, rushing, bumping, their rough, wool coats rubbing against him, their heavy suitcases knocking into him. He was turned this way and that. A leaf in a breeze.

He was lost. Alone.

He closed his eyes, tried to make the world go away. Hoped he wouldn't see the same thing he always saw when he closed his eyes.

His mother's smile, her face. Her voice calling to him.

Then: *the hem of his mother's black coat poking out of a pile of rubble.*

He opened his eyes again, shocked and surprised to find himself where he had been. That people were still all around him, ignoring him, abandoning him.

And then he saw the hand. A woman's hand. Soft. Friendly. Wanting to help. His heart began to beat faster, his blood to pound. It was his mother. She had found him. She wasn't dead after all. It was just her coat that he had seen, that was all. His mother had taken it off, she had survived, and she was here now. For him.

He blinked, and a wave of sadness surged through him as he realised that it wasn't his mother after all. He mustn't cry, he told himself, because that wasn't what boys did. They had to be strong. They had to keep mum.

Mum.

Not Mum, no. It was Miss Parkins standing in front of him, smiling. He liked Miss Parkins. She made him feel safe. She hadn't left him, hadn't abandoned him. She had come and found him.

He ran to her, taking her hand, pressing himself

against her. She smelled like flowers. She smelled lovely. And safe.

'Edward,' she was saying, 'I've got you. You wandered off . . .'

She reached down, stroked his hair. He thought of closing his eyes, but didn't.

She led him back to the rest of the group, who were still on the platform, waiting. The RAF captain was saying that their next train was delayed by a couple of hours, and his headmistress was looking at the pilot like it was his fault.

Around him, the rest of the children were quarrelling. Flora wanted something, and Miss Parkins, having checked Edward was all right, dropped his hand, went over to see what it was.

Edward looked at the ground. There was a frozen puddle with a big crack running through it. He could see the darkening sky in it, the clouds rolling in.

He thought of his mother and felt alone once more.

Transit

The children were tired. Their earlier, fidgety energy had dissipated, and in between bouts of napping they looked out of the window of the second train, seeing a night darker than any they had ever experienced in the city. Their thoughts were written on their faces. Eve could tell they were missing their families, and their homes. The journey was unsettling them, making them more wary about their final destination. It had stopped being an adventure.

Eve wasn't surprised. The train that they had eventually boarded was considerably more old-fashioned and primitive than the one they had taken out of King's Cross. It had wooden benches in place of upholstered seats, the windows were stained with smoke and oil, it clanked and creaked, and it was decidedly draughty. And to make matters worse, blackout regulations meant the train had to travel in complete darkness.

Eve looked round the carriage. In the moonlight, everyone's faces seemed pale and ghostlike. Edward was next to her, huddled into her body. He hadn't left her side since he had wandered off on the platform. The RAF captain, Harry Burstow, was in front of them. Eve caught sight of someone on the opposite side of the carriage.

A nurse.

Her breath caught as the nurse slowly turned her head and looked at her. The nurse's eyes and cheeks were shadowed holes, her skin so bleached out it looked like bone. Eve felt panic rise within her, sudden, sharp, and her hand went to her throat, holding on tightly to the cherub pendant she wore.

Eve's heart quickened, her breath shortened as she closed her eyes and saw ghosts from her past coming back to life. Unspooling before her eyes like an old monochrome newsreel. And she was back there in black and white. And red. So much red.

And pain. So many different kinds of pain . . .

No . . . no . . .

She closed her eyes tighter. Willed the memory away.

When she felt she could open them again, the nurse was looking out of the window. Eve took her fingers away from her throat, let the pendant fall back into place.

'Are you all right?' Harry leaned forward, concern on his face. 'You seemed to have a . . . turn.'

'I'm fine. Thank you.' She took a deep breath. Another. He was still looking at her.

'Can you stop that, please?' she said, feeling warm despite the cold in the carriage.

He frowned. 'Stop what?'

Eve swallowed hard. 'Looking at me.'

He gave a small laugh, looked around as if appealing to the moonlight. 'I can hardly see you.'

'Well . . .' Eve searched for something to say. 'Stop trying.' She found her smile, fixed it in place.

'I'm only wondering . . .' He had raised his eyebrow once more.

'Wondering what?'

'What you're hiding with that smile.'

Eve flinched, the memory of a few seconds

earlier flitting through her mind. 'This is my face for work,' she said, trying to make her voice match her smile.

Harry looked slightly put out. 'So you're not really smiling at me?'

Eve opened her mouth to answer, but couldn't think what to say without insulting him further. The truth was she liked him, liked the way his eyes crinkled at the corners when he smiled. The way he smoothed down his wavy blond hair when he thought she wasn't watching him. But she didn't like the way he focused on her, or the fact that he had seen such pain and fear on her face. And she knew she must never let him see it again.

He lit a cigarette and, in her peripheral vision Eve noticed Jean roll her eyes, shake her head.

Ignoring them both, she looked down at Edward. From her seat on the other side of the aisle, Flora had been smiling at him, and when he didn't return it she had then waved at him. But Edward didn't return the smile or the wave. He just stared at her. Expressionless.

It seemed like the skeleton of a station, picked clean and left to rot. The buildings were soot-blackened brick, the roof tiles were loose and missing, the windows broken, the wood rotten. A chill wind whistled through them, high-pitched flute-like. Discordant notes playing an unwelcome tune.

As the steam from the departing train melted into the mist of the night, Eve, Harry, Jean and the children huddled together for warmth on the platform as a limping figure, his outline weakly illuminated by the flicker of the oil lamp he held, made his slow way towards them.

Eve felt the children shrink away from the figure, gasp as he neared them. Even Jean had become tense.

His face loomed at them, out of the mist.

'Miss Hogg, I presume?' he said.

Jean bridled, stepped forward. Whatever fear she might have experienced at the man's approach had vanished. 'Mrs,' she said firmly, a hint of indignation in her voice.

The man laughed, gave a small bow of the head. 'Excuse me. Dr Jim Rhodes. Local education board.' Up close there was nothing scary about him. In fact he appeared quite avuncular.

The children, sensing no threat and seeing their

headmistress was dealing with things, relaxed slightly.

Eve felt a hand on her arm. She turned. Harry gestured to the road behind the station, then back to her.

'Nice meeting you, Miss Parkins. I'll . . . come and visit when I can.' His manner was formal but friendly, yet it seemed to Eve that there was more he wanted to say.

'Please,' said Eve, 'call me E—'

Jean gave Eve a stern look. 'Come on. We're already late for our bus.'

Eve followed her down the platform, then turned back. But it was too late. Harry had already gone. Just another brief encounter, she thought.

The bus was almost as ancient as the train.

It made its way from the station, headlights off, over the flat landscape. Clouds obscured the moon and stars. The whole of the countryside looked like it was smothered by a huge Army blanket.

Jim Rhodes drove with Fraser, Flora's little brother, sitting next to him. Out of all the children, he was the only one who hadn't been scared when Dr Rhodes limped out of the fog. Curious, but not scared.

'Why do you limp?' asked Fraser, sniffing and wiping his nose on his sleeve.

Eve leaned forward, touched the boy on the arm. 'Fraser . . .'

Jim Rhodes smiled. 'It's all right.' He glanced down at the boy, trying not to take his eyes off the darkened road. 'Got it in the last war. Too close to a shell.' He returned his attention to the road ahead of him. 'I was lucky.'

Eve sat back and looked out of the window. Her eyes had adjusted and she was able to pick out varying shades of black and grey. She realised they were coming into a village. She could make out winding, cobbled streets, stone cottages up ahead. She looked harder. Something was wrong. Something was missing.

There were no people.

Eve turned round as Joyce tugged her sleeve. 'Where is everybody?'

Joyce's eyes were wide open, head cocked to one side, quizzical. *Grown-ups have all the answers*, thought Eve. *Grown-ups know everything*. She sighed.

'Maybe . . .' Eve looked out of the window once more. 'Maybe the village was cleared. For the war.'

Joyce still wasn't convinced.

'Abandoned years ago,' said Jim Rhodes. 'Economy probably took a turn for the worse.'

'Or . . . or . . .' Fraser was jumping up and down in his seat. 'Or maybe everyone got the plague . . .'

The other children perked up at this, began to take an interest in their surroundings, preparing to voice their own theories. Eve knew how this would end and had opened her mouth to stop them when Jean beat her to it.

'That's enough. No more questions for the rest of the journey.'

The children fell silent immediately. Crisis averted. Jean's expression showed that the whole situation was Eve's fault for encouraging them. Eve ignored her.

Edward, still clinging to Eve, sensed the atmosphere between them and clung on harder, when there was a loud bang.

The bus rocked from side to side. The children screamed and hung on to their seats.

'Bugger!' Jim Rhodes stopped the bus, stood up in his seat and pointed out of the window.

'We've lost the tyre,' he said.

The bus listed to one side. Eve looked out of

the window. In place of a tyre was what looked like a huge dead slug.

'We're stuck here,' said Fraser.

It was hard to tell whether he was thrilled or terrified.

The Empty Village

The children pulled their coats around them and tightened their scarves. Huddled together outside the bus, teeth chattering, hands deep in pockets, none of them spoke. Eve noticed how Flora held Fraser close to her. The night was bitterly cold but, Eve thought, it was more than the cold that sent a chill through them all.

The village was eerily quiet. Empty. Not like London after the bombings, where there were still plenty of people around, trying to put their lives back together again, stumble on, go forward together. This was the opposite. The buildings were still here; it was the people who had gone. They seemed to be in a ghost town.

'Everyone stay close by . . .'

Eve turned. Jean was issuing an unnecessary order to the children. None of them had moved.

Behind her, Jim Rhodes gave the tyre a kick, then, swearing some more, but under his breath this time, he made his way towards the back of the bus.

'There's a spare in the boot,' he announced.

Jean walked in step with him. 'I'll give you a hand.'

Jim Rhodes stopped walking, stared at her. 'You?'

'I've changed many a wheel in my time.' Her eyes twinkled when she spoke, the corners of her mouth turned up, almost a smile. Jim Rhodes returned it. Slightly flustered, she turned to Edward, who was still attached to Eve's coat. She held out her hand. 'Edward. Why don't you help us?' It was less a question, more a command.

Edward just clung tighter to Eve.

Jean stood her ground, arm still outstretched. 'Come on. I'll show you how we change a tyre.'

He shook his head, clinging all the harder.

'I don't think he'll . . .' Eve began, then stopped.

Jean marched towards Edward, took his hand and pulled him away from her.

'He can't stay attached to you all the time,' she said, dragging the scared little boy away with her. 'Watch the other children, please.'

Concerned and a little scared herself, Eve walked round the side of the bus to where the children were huddled. They still hadn't moved and they were all staring at a field at the side of the road, eyes wide with fear and wonder. Eve hurried towards them, wondering what the source of their fascination could be. A sheep was looking right back at them.

'I never seen a sheep before . . .' Alfie sounded shocked.

Fraser frowned. 'Why's it staring at us?'

Flora, Eve noticed, had her eyes closed. 'Make it stop . . .'

Joyce turned to Eve, hands on hips, taking charge in the absence of Mrs Hogg. 'Miss, it's scaring the younger children.' Her tone of voice demanded that action be taken.

Eve smiled. 'It's only a sheep. It won't hurt you.'

She turned away from the children and the sheep. The village drew her attention. It rose out of the cold mist like a land-locked *Mary Celeste*.

Then she heard something. Faint, but unmistakable. The sound of . . . what was it? Voices? Yes. Singing. Coming from the village.

There were some empty cottages in front of her. They were old with sagging roofs, weeds climbing mildewed walls. One of the cottages, she noticed, was burned out, but there had been no attempt to knock the rest of it down or to patch it up. It had just been left. A broken metal sign hung off the front wall:

Mr Horatio Jerome M.S. Esq.,

Solicitor.

Eve could read it in the moonlight. Did the sound come from in there?

She listened. Yes. She thought that it did.

She looked at the burned-out house once more. And she felt something. Some pull, some . . . she couldn't explain it. Not even to herself. A fascination? A draw?

And there they were again. The voices. They were children's voices.

Eve looked back at the bus, at the children standing there. None of them was singing, and by now most of them were attempting to pet the sheep. Jean and Jim Rhodes were busy with the spare tyre and Edward was watching them. None of them appeared to have heard the voices.

Eve turned back to the burned-out cottage. To the village, frozen in the mist. She began to walk towards it.

Soon her shoes were echoing on the cobbles of the streets, as she reached the charred shell of the cottage. The whole front was missing, and the two windows above and the chasm below made it look like a screaming face. She shivered. Listened.

Children were singing again. The words were indistinct, carried on the wind, phasing in and out, but she could make out some of them. It was a nursery rhyme or lullaby.

'Jennet Humfrye lost her baby . . .'

She kept walking, the voices becoming louder, the words more discernible as she did so.

'Died on Sunday, seen on Monday . . .'

Eve reached the market square. Stopped.

'Who will die next? It must be YOU . . .'

The voices stopped, the final word echoing round the empty stone dwellings. Eve looked round, expecting to hear footsteps, running. Giggling, even, as the children sped off. Nothing. No one. She was alone in an empty place.

Then she heard something else. A sound. From one of the houses.

Eve turned to face it. This time there was no singing, no voices. Just movement.

'Hello?' she called as she walked slowly towards one of the ruined cottages and looked inside.

Although the window was filthy with years of accumulated dirt, she could just make out a small living room. The walls were damp, the meagre belongings dusty. It looked like the cottage had been abandoned in a hurry. Eve shivered again from more than just the cold.

And then a face appeared in front of her.

Eve screamed.

The Old Man

Eve fell back in shock, lost her footing and hit the cobbles. When she looked up, the face had gone.

Shakily, she stood up and this time she saw the outline of an old man cowering beneath the window. His hands were over his head, and he was whimpering.

'I'm sorry,' said Eve, speaking to him through the glass.

'Go away . . .' The old man rocked backwards and forwards.

'I didn't mean to startle you.'

He put one hand up, made a shooing motion. 'Get away. Get away. Before you see her . . .' He said more, but the words were lost as he began to mutter to himself.

'I'm not going to hurt you.'

The old man began to move.

'Please . . .' said Eve.

He straightened up, put his face to the glass, and Eve recoiled slightly. His eyes were huge and white, staring. Like two milky moons. He was blind.

Eve shivered. 'I'm sorry if I scared you.'

The old man seemed to be repeating Eve's words to himself. He put his head on one side. 'You sound sad,' he said.

Eve was slightly taken aback. 'I'm . . . I'm not sad.'

'You are. You're like *her*.' He raised his voice and his hand flew out in a gesture, pointing to someone neither of them could see.

'Who?' asked Eve. 'I'm like who?'

'Go away!' The old man slammed his fist against the filthy window. The glass shattered.

'Go away . . .' He slumped down, curling in on himself once more. His hands covered his head and he began to cry.

Eve looked back to the bus, then back to the old man. She didn't know what to do for the best. The old man was keening to himself, saying the same words over and over again.

'Go away . . . go away . . .'

Holding her breath and trying not to cry herself, Eve hurried back to the bus as quickly as she could.

Nine Lives Causeway

'Look! Look! That's a Lancaster bomber! And that's a Halifax! And a Spitfire! And . . .' Alfie turned to Eve. 'Can we go and see them, please, Miss? Please?'

'Sit down, Alfie.' Jean spoke before Eve could answer.

The boy sat down, a hurt expression on his face.

Eve looked out of the bus's grimy window at the same silhouettes of planes that Alfie had seen, the same glow of red lights. But she didn't see them. All she saw was an airman. A handsome captain in his RAF uniform. She remembered his good humour, his easy smile. How he had made her feel. And she smiled.

*

The mist thickened, became a curling, rolling, almost living entity. Within a few seconds it had completely engulfed the bus.

Jim Rhodes concentrated on the narrow strip of road ahead of him.

'Where are we?' asked Eve.

'Nine Lives Causeway,' he said, still peering ahead. 'Don't worry about this, it's just a sea fret. I'm used to it.'

Eve could hear something under the rumbling of the engine. A whispering, susurrating noise.

'What's that?' she asked. 'Can you hear it?'

'Hear what?' said Jim Rhodes.

'A kind of . . . I don't know. Swirling noise. Swishing. Sliding.'

'Must be the eels,' Jim Rhodes said. 'They live under the water.'

Eve felt a lurch of fear. She had never liked eels.

He saw her expression, gave a sharp, barking laugh. 'Or the tyres on the wet road. Take your pick.'

'Shouldn't you put your headlights on?' asked Jean.

Eve noticed there was an edge of tension to her voice that she was struggling to control.

'Can't do that, sorry,' Jim Rhodes said. 'Blackout rules still apply here.'

'But . . . but . . .' Jean was staring out of the window, apparently transfixed by the wet, choking mist. 'We could come off the road . . .'

'We could also be underneath a German bomber.'

A tense silence fell as they all found something else to worry about.

Eve looked for Edward and noticed he was sitting at the back of the bus next to Flora, who was holding his hand.

She turned her attention back to the outside world, just in time to see a cross jutting out of the mud by the side of the bus. She was going to ask Jim Rhodes about it but immediately forgot as, rising out of the mist right before them, she saw a huge old mansion.

Jim Rhodes breathed a sigh of relief.

'Welcome to Eel Marsh House,' he said.

Eel Marsh House

Ominous and desolate were the two words that came into Eve's mind as she stared up at the front of Eel Marsh House. It stood imposing and resolute, an ancient monolith from a previous age, wreathed in mist and fog, like the last standing tombstone in a decaying and crumbling cemetery.

She stepped backwards, tripping over a thick black cable.

'Careful,' said Jim Rhodes, catching her. 'There's an outhouse round the side where we've put the generator.' He pointed to the cable.

Jean had been walking around, familiarising herself with the new surroundings. 'Look at that,' she said now, pointing to the perimeter of the grounds. 'Barbed wire.' She turned back to him. 'Is that really necessary?'

Jim Rhodes shrugged. 'Nothing to do with me. Home Guard put it there.'

'To keep the Germans out, or us in?'

Jim Rhodes sighed as he shepherded the children towards the house. Glancing uneasily at the barbed wire, Eve followed him.

Eel Marsh House looked no better from the inside. If anything, it looked worse. No one had lived in it for decades – possibly not even this century – and it had clearly been left to decay. The paint on the woodwork was blistered and mildewed, the paper on the walls torn and peeling. Old, rusted oil lamps stuck out of the walls, cobwebbed and disused. Patches of black mould were everywhere, like the darkness outside was trying to get in. The walls felt wet to the touch, the air was chilled, and the damp made Eve's skin itch and prickle. It was a place she knew she could never be warm in.

The thick black cables she had stumbled over in the driveway outside were everywhere. Snaking up the walls, connected to dusty bulbs, bringing a dim, flickering illumination to the house when Jim Rhodes flicked the switch.

Eve and Jean stood before the big central staircase and looked round. Both were speechless.

Jim Rhodes nodded, misreading their expressions of horror for ones of amazement. 'Big, isn't it?' he said.

Neither of them answered. The children, huddled behind them, were also peering around.

Jim Rhodes walked over to a set of old wooden double doors and tried to pull them open. The wood was so damp and warped that it took him several attempts, but eventually he managed it. Inside the room, two rows of made-up wrought-iron beds were facing each other. All were unoccupied.

'Children's quarters,' he said.

Jean scanned the hall, glanced into the children's room, then back to Jim Rhodes. 'Where are the others?'

Jim Rhodes frowned. 'Others?'

Jean looked exasperated. 'The others. The other school parties.'

'Oh,' he said. 'They don't arrive until next week. You're the first.' He smiled, as if this made them special.

'And you expect us to live like this?'

Jim Rhodes shrugged, looked apologetic. 'Well, it's . . .'

'Derelict is what it is, Dr Rhodes,' said Jean. She moved up close to him, her voice dropping. Eve knew that was never a good sign. 'My husband is a brigadier in the Army and he wouldn't let his men stay in a place like this, let alone a group of children.'

Jim Rhodes put his hands up in a gesture of supplication — or perhaps surrender, Eve wasn't sure which. 'Granted, it . . . it hasn't been lived in for a long while, but I'm sure once the place is . . . is full of people it'll . . . it will come back to life.' He nodded, as if trying to convince himself.

Jean was clearly unimpressed. 'That's not good enough, Dr Rhodes.'

Steel entered Jim Rhodes's voice. 'It's all we have, Mrs Hogg.'

Eve was aware that the children had gathered around and were watching the grown-ups argue. She turned to them, smile in place. 'Come on, children, let's unpack.'

Tom didn't move. 'Can't we look around?'

Eve's smile stayed fixed. 'First we unpack.'

'But . . .'

'Where are all the other children?' Joyce asked, her voice wobbling with concern.

Eve opened her mouth to reply, but Jean spoke first.

'Enough.'

They all stopped talking.

'Eve, have Dr Rhodes show you around. I'll sort out the children,' Jean ordered.

'Yes, Headmistress,' said Eve, feeling, not for the first time, that she was one of the children and not their teacher. Jean often made her feel like that. It was something that annoyed Eve, but she knew what Jean's reaction would be if she ever dared complain.

She looked at Jim Rhodes, and together they began their tour of the house.

In the Nursery

'Through there is the kitchen,' said Jim Rhodes, gesturing to a doorway off to their left, 'and the dining room is out the back.'

Eve nodded, taking it all in.

He stopped suddenly and tried to look at her but couldn't keep his eyes on her face. He sighed. 'I'm . . . sorry they didn't tell you what it was going to be like.'

'That's quite all right, Doctor,' Eve said softly. 'I realise you're just the messenger.'

He gave her a small smile, glanced back down the hallway. 'Thank you. I wish everyone was as understanding.'

'Mrs Hogg . . . takes her duties very seriously. She has a responsible position with the children and believes in rolling up her sleeves and getting on with it. She means well.'

'That's one way of looking at it.'

'Is there another way?'

'Yes. People like Mrs Hogg put all their feelings and emotions away in a box. They tell themselves they're being rational. That's what the war does to some people. Their way of coping, I suppose.'

'And how do you know this?'

Jim Rhodes sighed. 'I saw it last time. Plenty of fellows had that attitude and not many of them made it home, I'm afraid. They meant well, too.' He paused. 'Upstairs?'

Eve looked at the staircase. It was old, heavy and sturdy-looking, but she wondered what state it was actually in.

'There's two rooms for yourself and Mrs Hogg,' he said. 'We'll get the rest fixed up when more people arrive.'

He gestured for her to go upstairs. She did so, conscious of him limping behind her, conscious too of the boards creaking and groaning with every step.

'What are you a doctor of, if you don't mind me asking?'

By this time the staircase was wide enough for Jim Rhodes to walk alongside her. 'Medicine,' he said.

'But you work for the education board?'

'I'm also an air warden,' he pointed out, a little defensively. 'We do what we can.'

The first floor appeared even less cared for than downstairs. Jim Rhodes took out a torch, switched it on.

'No lights up here yet, I'm afraid, but there's plenty of candles and oil lamps.'

His enforced bonhomie was wearing slightly thin, Eve thought. They stopped in front of two doorways, one either side of the hall.

'These two are your rooms. We'll keep the other bedrooms locked until the rest arrive.'

Eve looked along the end of the corridor. One door was open.

'All of them?' she asked.

Jim Rhodes followed her gaze. Frowned. 'Oh. I thought I'd locked them all.'

He turned away, dismissing it, but Eve was curious. Something about the doorway seemed to be calling to her, inviting her in. She took the torch and walked down the hallway, Jim Rhodes following slowly behind.

'I think this used to be a nursery,' Jim said.

Eve shone the torch on the walls, illuminating several layers of peeling wallpaper, rather like the rings of a tree. She could date the age of the house by the amount of paper on the walls. She stopped moving, feeling something. Something that she couldn't put her finger on.

She shivered. 'It's so . . . cold in here.'

'We only had enough heaters for downstairs,' he said.

She hugged herself, walked to the window, looked out. She could make out a forest in the mist, surrounding the house. The moon above the mist was high and clear in the sky, casting her shadow on the wall behind her.

'I didn't mean cold, Dr Rhodes, I didn't mean that. It feels . . .' She took a breath. Closed her eyes. It was like there was a thought, an important thought, just out of reach of her mind. Or a feeling that she couldn't quite describe. She remembered the empty Underground tunnel she'd sheltered in when she'd been in London. Dark. Hollow. 'I don't know. It feels . . . sad,' she said, feeling the cherub pendant around her neck.

Jim came and stood next to her by the window. 'Rooms aren't sad, Miss Parkins. People are.'

Eve continued to look outside at the misty, frozen world beneath them.

'Come on,' he said. 'I'll lock this behind us.'

At his words, Eve took a deep breath and followed him out of the room.

But her shadow stayed exactly where it was.

It turned its head, watched them leave.

The Night

Outside Eel Marsh House, the mist still encased the sky and the sea in a thick grey shroud. Jim shook Eve's hand.

'I'll try and get all the repairs done as soon as I can.'

'Thank you,' Eve said, taking in his stooped figure, thinking how much older he appeared suddenly.

Jim Rhodes looked around, at the house, the grounds, the driveway, then back at Eve. Something seemed to be on his mind, something he was unable, or unwilling, to express. 'It's a big place,' he said hesitantly. 'You'll . . . you'll have to keep a close watch on the children.'

'Of course,' she said.

'Keep them away from the causeway, I mean. The tide can come in very quickly and you've seen how those sea frets can—'

Eve placed her hand gently on his arm. 'Doctor, we'll be fine.'

Reluctantly, he returned her smile. 'Yes, of course. Sorry.' His smile faded as he saw Jean Hogg appear in the doorway.

'I'd best be off. Get over the causeway while I still can. Good luck, ladies,' he called as he hurried back to the bus.

Together Jean and Eve watched him walk away.

'He's not heard the last from me.' Jean's eyes were blazing with righteous anger.

Eve knew what was coming next. She had been on the receiving end of her moral diatribes before. 'I didn't know your husband was in the Army,' she said.

Jean frowned. 'Why would you?'

Presuming the question was rhetorical, Eve didn't reply. Back in London, Jean's private and work life were kept as two distinct and separate entities. Clearly things were going to be the same here, too.

'Come on,' Jean said. 'We'd better start cleaning.'

'What, now? Shouldn't we be putting the children to bed?'

'Nonsense. They can help us.'

Eve must have clearly been surprised because Jean felt the need to elaborate.

'They'll be too excited to sleep. And besides, a bit of hard work never killed anyone.'

She walked back into the house, her back ramrod-straight as usual, giving no indication that she had recently undertaken hours of tiring travelling. Eve shook her head and followed her inside.

Prayers

The children were exhausted.

They were kneeling by their beds, dressed in their night clothes, eyes tight shut. Eve and Jean were watching over them.

They had all worked hard. Everyone had been given tasks and they had carried them out with military precision. Eve had sneaked a few glances at Jean as they had been working and the look of pride in her eyes was unmistakable.

Buckets and pans were placed underneath leaks, the floors were swept, the surfaces dusted. For her part, Eve had taken a cloth and tried to scrub off the patches of mould that were growing all over the place, thick and black and as dark as shadows. But it didn't work. No matter how hard she tried, how much elbow grease she put into it, the mould refused to budge.

Sometimes, it seemed to be growing while she watched. Or, rather, didn't watch. She would look at the wall, catch the mould from the corners of her eyes, and see it move, expand. The same way she had looked directly up at the night sky and seen whole constellations suddenly reveal themselves in her peripheral vision. Then she would focus on the mould itself and it would be exactly the same as it had been before. Or it seemed to be. She sighed. Maybe just a trick of the light. And the fact that she was very, very tired.

'There are four corners to my bed . . .'

The children all spoke with one voice, mouthing the words to the prayer in their usual sing-song fashion.

'Four angels round my head . . . One to watch and one to pray . . .'

All speaking except one, Eve noticed.

'And two to bear my soul away.'

Edward was kneeling with the rest of them, his hands together, his eyes tight shut. Eve wondered what he was praying for, or whether he was even praying at all. She knew what he was thinking, or, rather, who he was thinking about.

Jean clapped her hands together. 'Come along, children, everybody into their beds.'

They all did as they were told, and Eve went round tucking them all in, checking that they were all right. She stopped by Edward's bed, knelt down beside him.

'Look,' she said. 'If you don't want to speak yet, that's fine. You take your time.'

Edward, of course, just stared up at her.

Eve leaned forwards, feeling that familiar emptiness inside herself, that painful ache of separation. Knowing how he must feel.

She closed her eyes. Saw the nurse from the train. Remembered her terror.

'Your mummy will always be with you,' she said to Edward. 'The people we lose never leave us completely. Believe me . . .'

Edward reached out and took her hand. Eve was so surprised she felt tears welling. She had reached him. At last.

'Now,' she said, 'promise me you're going to sleep well tonight. No bad dreams.'

Edward nodded, his body small and slight under the bedclothes.

'Do you know what a nightmare is?' Eve continued. 'It's your mind's way of letting go of all the bad thoughts. Once you've dreamed them, they're gone.'

Edward reached over to his bedside table, found some paper and a piece of charcoal. He wrote something on the paper, handed it over to Eve. She looked at it.

That's rubbish, it read.

Eve laughed. 'Oh, is it?'

But Edward was already writing another message. Eve waited patiently for him to finish and pass it over.

Mummy says you fight bad dreams with good thoughts.

'Well, you try that then, right?' She smiled once more.

Edward nodded, returned the smile.

Jean had noticed Eve talking to Edward and now came over to check what was happening.

'We'll get you talking again tomorrow, won't we, Edward?' she said, her back perfectly stiff, her face stern. 'Can't have this nonsense going on too long.'

The smile vanished from Edward's face.

Eve stood up, but Edward had grabbed her arm, not wanting to let her go. Jean bent down and firmly removed Edward's hand.

'There's a good boy,' she said, with a brittle smile, leading Eve away from him, towards the bedroom doors. 'He needs to learn.'

Eve thought of what Jim Rhodes had said, how some people put their emotions in a box and closed them off, thinking they were doing the right thing. Was this really the best way to treat children? she wondered. And would this help Edward to come to terms with his loss? Or would it make him feel it even more acutely?

'Sleep well, everyone,' Jean said from the doorway.

Turning off the light switch, she plunged the room into darkness.

The Outhouse

Eve had just one last task to do before she could sleep. Jean had said she would be perfectly happy to do it, but Eve could see how tired she looked, despite her protestations. So this was how, shivering in the freezing cold, Eve found herself walking towards the outhouse, a rumbling, pulsing noise in the air, torch in hand.

The grass had been cut back in preparation for their arrival, but the ground was still uneven, roots and stones waiting to catch the unwary, testament to the years of neglect.

She reached the outhouse, went inside. The rumbling, pulsing noise was immediately much louder. The generator was old, battered and oily. It took up most of the room, grinding out electricity for the house. She played the beam of her torch across the front of the machine, found what she was looking for, flicked the switch. The generator began to power down.

Eve straightened up. And froze.

She felt a muscle spasm between her shoulder blades, an unease in her body. She moved her arms trying to relieve it, expel it. No good. She knew it for what it was: the distinct sensation that someone was watching her.

She tried to rationalise it, work out who it could be. One of the children, probably. Couldn't sleep and followed her out. Edward, perhaps, upset. Or Tom, playing a trick on her. It was just the sort of thing that boy would do.

She turned quickly, hoping to catch them out. No one there. She listened. Nothing but the cooling tick of the motor before her. She looked through the outhouse window, glancing left and right, seeing only mist, the night.

She turned back to the generator. It had stopped completely now. She listened once more. Nothing. Squaring her still-tightened shoulders, determined to be brave, she turned, left the outhouse, walked back to the house.

In the distance a woman stood, her figure silhouetted against the vast misty sky, against the darkness.

Watching.

Waiting.

The Cherub

Once inside, Eve locked the front door behind her and pocketed the key. If there was a child out there now, playing their silly tricks, it would serve them right. Then she told herself off for even thinking such a heartless thing. She opened one of the double doors leading to their quarters and looked in on them. All present and correct. Relieved, she made her way up to bed.

Her room was illuminated only by candles. Eve had unpacked her meagre possessions from her suitcase, hanging what few clothes she had in the wardrobe. A diary, which she placed on the bedside table, and a couple of pieces of inexpensive, but sentimentally valued, jewellery completed her belongings.

She carefully took off the cherub necklace and kissed it, placing it down on the bedside table beside the diary. She gave out a sad-sounding sigh as she looked at it. Her smile was the next thing to be removed. There was no one there she needed to smile for. She stared at herself in a small compact mirror. *I look tired*, she thought. *Tired*.

She got into bed and found it to be almost as cold and damp as the rest of the house. She tried not to shiver, to relax, but her eyes wouldn't close, sleep wouldn't come. She lay on her back, staring at the ceiling. There was a patch of mould above her bed. It looked like an island. She tried to imagine what it would be like. Some distant place with palm trees and sandy beaches stretching as far as the eye could see. The kind of place she had seen only in Hollywood films. As she looked at the damp patch, part of her, the honest part, wished she was there, in the warm sun, not a care in the world. No war, no unhappiness. Somewhere she could relax. Where she could smile because she meant it.

However, sleep still eluded her, so she rolled over on to her side and stared at the window. She could hear the sea behind the blackout blinds, but knew it wasn't lapping on her tropical shore. It was cold, harsh, splashing against the causeway. She imagined the eels in the water, slithering and sliding round each other, over each other, curling round the island itself.

Restless, she turned over on to her other side.

And found herself in a different room.

She looked round, eyes wide with shock. Her bed was now one of many, a whole row of them stretching away to a set of double doors. All the other beds were empty. It was a hospital ward. Empty of patients but full of shadows. She could hear faint screams echoing in the distance.

Her heart pounding, her mind reeling, trying desperately to take in what had just happened, she pushed back the covers, put her feet to the floor, got up. She walked past the other beds, searching for the source of the screaming. They were all empty but unmade, the outline of departed patients still visible in each of them.

Her bare feet made slapping echoes on the cold, tiled floor as she walked through the ward.

The screaming increased as she reached the double doors. She pushed them open, approached the single doorway beyond. The screams were now agonisingly, painfully loud, almost unbearably so.

She put her hand to the door. Hesitated. No matter how much she wanted to look inside, fear of what she would see stopped her. She stretched out her hand once more. The same thing happened; her hand wouldn't make the connection. She took a deep breath, another. And, pushing the fear away, opened the door.

Before her was a flurry of doctors and nurses, all surrounding a woman lying on a bed. She was the source of the screaming and there was blood everywhere. She was giving birth.

Eve leaned in, trying to see the woman's face, but the medical staff were in the way. All she could make out was her hand clutching the metal side of the bed.

Then everything changed. The woman stopped screaming, started panting, as if she had just finished running a marathon. A nurse stepped away from the bed, carrying a bundle of blanket. Eve craned her neck to see as a tiny hand emerged from it, the miniature fingers grasping, flexing.

'Let me see him . . . Please . . .'

It was the mother, calling from the bed. But the nurse paid her no heed. She kept the blanket-wrapped bundle close to her body as she turned and pushed past Eve and through the door.

'Please,' called the mother, 'please, come back . . .'

The nurse didn't even acknowledge her. She just kept walking, the door swinging behind her, creaking and cracking but refusing to close.

'Please . . .' The mother's voice was becoming more desperate, catching in her throat as she called. 'Don't go, please, let me see . . .'

But there was no reply, just the door swinging backwards and forwards.

Creak . . . crack . . . Creak . . . crack . . .

Eve tried to ignore the noise and concentrate on the voice. There was something familiar about it. She moved in to get a closer look at the mother. And saw who was lying in the bed.

Herself.

Creak . . . Crack . . .

Eve gasped and sat bolt upright, breathing raggedly. She was back in her bedroom in Eel Marsh House. Alone. She shook her head, trying to dislodge the images that she had carried over from sleep. *It was a dream, that's all. Just a dream.*

As her breathing returned to normal, she lay down once more, intending to go back to sleep, but something stopped her. A sound, rhythmic, pulsing.

It's the door, she thought, in the hospital. Still swinging, still refusing to close. She looked at the bedroom door. It was closed. But the noise was still there.

Creak . . . crack . . . Creak . . . crack . . .

It must be the generator. Somehow it must have turned itself back on again. Even as she thought it, she knew it wasn't possible. She had turned it off herself. She listened again.

Creak . . . crack . . . Creak . . . crack . . .

Eve didn't feel the slightest bit sleepy. The dream had seen to that. She got out of bed and opened the blackout curtains. Nothing but an empty beach and a calm sea.

She heard the noise again. It was coming from inside the house.

Someone else must have heard it. She couldn't be the only one.

Creak . . . crack . . . Creak . . . crack . . .

Eve knew she couldn't count on someone else hearing it and acting on it. There were children in the house, and they were her responsibility. She would have to investigate it for herself. She lit a candle and opened the door. After a couple of deep breaths, still feeling the dream's adrenalin running round her system, she made her way into the hallway.

It was deserted. Eve crossed to Jean's room, put her ear to the door and listened. Heard only light snoring. The other noise was still there, coming from downstairs.

The children. That was it: they were getting up to a bit of midnight exploring. She would go down, have a quiet word and be back in bed before Jean woke up. Her headmistress would be none the wiser.

Cupping a hand round the candle flame, she made her way downstairs. The flame cast huge shadows on the walls. The black mould seemed to suck the shadows in, making them even darker.

She stopped at the children's quarters, crept into the room as quietly as she could. They were all there, sleeping.

And still she could hear the noise. *Why am I the only one who can hear it?* she thought. *Why hasn't it woken anyone else?*

Eve closed the door and made her way towards the kitchen. The sound was louder in there. She swung her candle round, trying to illuminate the dark corners. Saw nothing. No movement at all. She listened.

Creak . . . crack . . . Creak . . . crack . . .

The door at the other end of the kitchen was slightly ajar. Her heart hammering, Eve walked towards it.

It led to an old, narrow, stone staircase. Eve pushed it open and began to walk down, her candle flickering in the darkness. She was wary of falling, the stone slippery and damp under her feet, but she reached the bottom safely. Ahead of her was another door: old, rotting, almost black with mould. The sound was definitely coming from behind that.

Am I still dreaming? she wondered. *Going through door after door chasing a sound? To find . . .* She shuddered, feeling the chill, the damp. No. This was no dream. This was real.

Eve cleared her throat. 'Who's there?'

No reply.

'Is that . . . is that you, Dr Rhodes? Are you . . . do you need a bed for the night? Please . . . please tell me.'

Silence. There would be no going back now. Eve opened the door.

The smell hit her like a physical presence. The air was thick with a fetid, rank dampness. It permeated the foundations of the house with the stench of rot and decay. She clamped her hand over her mouth and nose, tried not to breathe it in. But she felt it, even in the short time she had been there, tainting her nightdress, sinking into the pores of her skin.

The room was huge. It probably covered the same area as the house, Eve guessed. The walls were stone, crumbling away and covered in moss. Water slowly trickled down them on to the wet floor, making the whole room glisten green and eerie in the candlelight.

There were rows and rows of shelves piled high with boxes, the lids pushed back, all crammed with old objects and artefacts, the damp and dusty remnants of the previous owners.

But Eve was alone.

Slowly taking her hand away from her face to cup the candle's flame, she shone the light around once more, crossing to the shelves. The boxes were wet with mildew. She managed to get the lid off one and looked inside. There was a jumble of paperwork and shabby, moth-eaten clothes. She replaced the lid and looked at the next box along. It was full of old toys, soaked, blackened and neglected. The faces of ancient dolls, now with sightless eyes and frozen, vacant smiles, stared at her. Underneath them was a wooden frame. What was left of the material draped over and round it was rotted and black, but Eve could just make out echoes of colour on it, enough to recognise what it had been. A puppet show. Feeling a pang of sadness and regret, she replaced the box. Childhood's end.

Next to the box of toys was something more interesting. An old phonograph. She reached out, touched the rusty machine. Was this what had been making the sound? She flicked the switch at its side, waited. Nothing happened. There were some cylinders next to it with writing on the side. She picked up the first one — *Alice Drablow* — and next to the name, some dates.

Then Eve saw something else. She frowned, brought the light in closer. It was beyond the shelf, on the stone wall itself. She held the candle up to it. There were words scratched into the stone, distressed, strangely angular letters: *MY GRIEF WILL LIVE IN THESE WALLS FOR EVER*.

Eve reached out, ran her fingers along the words. She wanted to get a feel for the letters, an impression of both them and who might have made them. But the stone was so damp and old that it crumbled at her touch. The words disappeared like they had been written in water, leaving Eve with a feeling of desolation and sadness, just like she had experienced in the nursery.

She stepped back, and knocked into something solid. She jumped, turned.

Creak . . . crack . . . Creak . . . crack . . .

An old rocking chair.

Was that what had been making the noise? Had someone been sitting in it? Rocking it? If that was the case, who was it and where were they now? As far as she could make out there was only one door, the one she had entered by. Did that mean whoever it had been was still down here with her?

Slowly, her heart hammering, she moved the candle round, trying to peer into the shadows.

A movement in the corner.

'Hello?'

The noise came again. From behind the next shelf along.

'Hello?' she repeated, hoping her voice sounded more confident than she felt.

She held her breath as she walked towards the sound. She stretched out her arm holding the candle and, wanting to see what was there but scared to get too near, looked along the shelf.

A rat came scuttling towards her.

Eve screamed and dropped the candle. It went out with a hiss as it hit the wet floor, throwing the room into darkness. She stood stock-still, breathing heavily. She could still hear the rat scurrying about somewhere.

And then she heard it.

Creak . . . crack . . . Creak . . . crack . . .

The rocking chair was moving again.

Eve made for the door. Running up the stairs as fast as she could in the pitch-black, slipping and sliding as she went, into the kitchen, straight up the main staircase and back into bed. She pulled the covers right over her head and lay there tense and rigid, more afraid than she had ever been in her life.

All she could hear was the waves crashing against the shore outside.

And the frantic beating of her terrified heart.

The Next Day

Things looked better the next morning.

The sun, bright and distant, had burned away the mist, leaving the sky a cloudless robin's-egg blue. Frost glittered and glistened everywhere. It was, thought Eve, the kind of morning you never experienced in a city.

She stood in the garden with Jean, watching the children. The garden might have seen better days and the barbed wire surrounding it was a constant reminder that the war was never really far away, but for the moment the children didn't seem to care. The girls were skipping along to 'Ring a Ring o' Roses' while Alfie and Fraser were chasing each other. Their laughter and happy energy chased away Eve's fears from the previous night like the sun dispersing the mist.

'Where's Edward?' asked Eve.

Jean kept her eyes on the children. 'I told him he can't come out until he's willing to speak.'

Eve didn't reply. She just turned, and made her way back to the house.

'Leave him be,' said Jean, her voice full of irritation.

Eve stopped. 'I'm going to set up my classroom for the lesson.'

There was nothing in that statement for Jean to argue with, so she contented herself with a curt nod, and Eve went back into the house.

As she made her way towards the dining room, Tom came hurtling round a corner, straight into her side, almost knocking Eve off her feet. She was just recovering when James did the same thing. Both boys stopped dead, breathless and guilty.

She rearranged herself and looked down at them.

'What are you doing?'

'Tag, Miss,' said Tom. 'James was It.'

'You shouldn't be running around.' She was about to say more when she noticed the doors to the children's quarters were open. Edward was sitting on his bed, drawing. It looked like he was in another world, on a lonely little planet with only one inhabitant.

'James,' said Eve, 'you used to be best friends with Edward, didn't you?'

James was about to answer, but Tom gave him a severe look and surreptitiously stamped on his foot. Eve noticed.

'Look, I know things have changed, James, but I'd like you to include him.' Her words encompassed Tom, too. 'It's times like this when he needs friends. Do you understand?'

The boys nodded.

'Just think if it was the other way round.'

She walked off, hoping they were thinking exactly that.

Tom

Tom knew Miss Parkins didn't like him. She didn't have to say it; she made it perfectly clear without words. He didn't know why. She just didn't. But that was fine, really, because he didn't like her. Or at least that was what he told himself.

Mrs Hogg was all right, though. She was strong. She had discipline. Although he'd had the cane from her a few times, she was never cruel. It had hurt, but not too much. She was hard but fair, and that was something Tom could respond to, respect, because that was the way things should be. His dad had told him that before he had left. Off to fight, his mother had said, been fighting all his life. That, thought Tom, was how a man should be. And his dad was a lot more forceful than Mrs Hogg when he was dishing out punishment, too. No mistake.

So he didn't care whether Miss Parkins, with her nice smile and her gentle manners, liked him or not. Didn't care at all. Not a bit. No. But he still found himself back in the children's quarters, doing what she had asked him to.

Edward didn't look up when Tom and James entered the room. He sat on his bed, head down, concentrating on his drawing. Tom moved closer, looking down over his shoulder. Edward was sketching a picture of a woman and a small boy, standing in front of a house. Tom felt a new kind of emotion inside. Sadness, anger, jealousy, compassion? He wasn't sure what it was. But it was there, and he didn't like it. It made him angry.

He stood there, waiting for Edward to acknowledge them. When he didn't, Tom said, 'Come on, Edward, let's go and explore.' He pulled him by the shoulder, but Edward didn't move, just slowly shook his head.

Tom was finding this difficult. He gave Edward's shoulder a punch. Just a light one. 'What's the matter? Don't you want to be friends?'

Edward flinched, put his head down, as if he were about to be hit. Any answer would be the wrong one.

Tom was getting irritated and it was starting to show. 'You've got to. Miss said.'

Panic was rising in Edward's eyes. He looked between the other two. James stepped forward, his voice quiet, compassionate. He smiled at his friend. 'Don't worry, it'll be all right. We're all stuck here, we've got to be friends.'

Tom saw how reassured Edward was by the words. Why couldn't he be the one the other children liked and got on with? He felt his anger rising further. He knew the pattern. He would soon need an outlet, something to vent it on. Something, hopefully, that would make the others respect him.

He grabbed Edward's drawing away from him.

Edward looked up, terrified, like a treasured possession, something of vital importance, had been stolen. He grabbed for it, but Tom moved it out of the way.

That was better, thought Tom. If he couldn't do something to get a good reaction, a bad one would do.

'I'll give it back,' he said, enjoying the power over the other boy, 'if you do what we say.'

Edward looked at James, who seemed uncomfortable and couldn't hold his gaze. Edward, having no choice, nodded.

Tom smiled and, Edward's drawing in hand, he walked into the hall. The other two followed him. He made straight for the stairs, started to run up them.

'Why don't you talk?' Tom said.

Edward didn't reply.

An idea came to Tom. 'I think . . . I think we should make you talk. Then Miss Parkins will like us.'

He turned to James, who didn't look happy about going along with Tom but nevertheless said nothing. Then he remembered: Miss Parkins already liked James. And the thought of that made him angry once more. He reached the landing and, not waiting for the other two, walked along the corridor, trying all the door handles, looking for an open one.

He found it.

The Poker

The room was dusty and empty. It had been cleared of furniture and all that remained was a black, soot-stained fireplace with a heavy iron grate placed in front of it.

Tom was disappointed and angry, as if the room had been emptied just to annoy him personally. 'There's nothing in here,' he called to the other two.

James and Edward entered the room, looked round. Tom was already voicing his displeasure about how boring the room was, when James heard something. He held up his hand, telling Tom to be quiet.

Tom didn't like being told what to do, and was

about to complain further when James told him to be quiet once again. And then he heard it too. A scratching sound; faint, but audible. Coming from the fireplace.

Edward, who hadn't fully committed to entering the room and was standing in the doorway, turned to leave. Tom wasn't going to allow that to happen.

'Oi,' he said, 'help us.' He grabbed hold of Edward and dragged him over to the fireplace, where Edward just stood and stared. He didn't seem interested in what the other two were doing, just waiting to have his drawing returned to him.

The scratching didn't stop.

Gesturing to James to do likewise, Tom knelt down and began to lift up the grate. It was too heavy, even for both of them, so Tom looked once more at Edward.

'Come on, don't just stand there.'

Edward, knowing a threat when he heard one, knelt down and joined them.

Together, they managed to lift off the grate, put it at the side of the fireplace. All three of them peered inside.

There was a dead crow lying curled and still in a nest, surrounded by several dead little chicks.

Edward and James scuttled back, recoiling from the sight, but Tom continued to stare, fascinated. The crow had clearly been there for a while because it had started to decay; its body decomposing from inside, almost mummified. The chicks just looked peaceful, like they were asleep.

Tom was transfixed. He loved being close to death, was fascinated by it. The war had been a godsend for Tom. While other children were terrified of the bombing, he loved it. He didn't know what would be left when he emerged the next morning or who would be missing. He always hoped that if someone he knew had been bombed, they would die messily and he would get to see the bloody body.

He reached for the poker at the side of the fireplace and gingerly began to examine the dead bird, prodding and poking it.

The crow's head came off.

The other two winced, turning their faces away. But Tom, enthralled, kept going. Having prodded some more and exhausted the possibilities of the mother, he turned his attention to the chicks.

'Don't, Tom . . .' James said.

'Shut up,' hissed Tom. He nudged one of the chicks gently with the poker.

And it moved.

The three boys – even Edward – called out in surprise, and they all scurried away from it.

But, slowly, they returned. Tom's fascination seemed to have infected the other two.

Tom frowned. 'What shall we do with it?' For once, he genuinely seemed not to have the answer.

James did, though. 'We should take it to Miss.'

Tom shook his head. 'But its mother is dead.'

'So?'

While the other two were arguing, Edward looked down at the tiny bird. A dead mother. An orphan. He would look after it. He would see that no harm came to it.

He reached out his hands to pick up the tiny chick, getting ready to welcome it, nurture it. But he didn't get that far. Tom brought the poker down, hard. The chick was now as dead as the rest of them.

Edward glared at Tom. James's mouth had dropped open. Tom's eyes darted between the two of them.

'What?' he said. His voice was shaky, but he was determined to justify himself. 'It . . . it was going to die anyway . . .' He laughed, pleased that he had shocked them into a reaction. It might have been a bit much, but it was better than being ignored. 'Oh, come on . . .'

Judging by their expressions, James and Edward didn't agree. Tom had had enough of them. He threw the poker down on the floor, suddenly tired of the whole thing, and turned to leave the room.

'Come on,' he said, pulling James with him.

Edward stayed where he was, watching them leave. Angry, lonely tears forming in his eyes.

Hide-and-Seek

Tom strode from the room, eyes ablaze. Killing the bird made him feel like he was capable of anything and no one could stop him. No one. He scanned the corridor, fists clenching and unclenching, teeth bared, looking for what he could do next.

He didn't get far.

Edward cannoned out of the room, mouth open, silently roaring, launching himself at Tom's back. Taken by surprise, Tom lost his footing and tumbled on to the floor.

Edward, shocked by his own actions, stopped dead and stared at Tom, who slowly got to his feet. James was rooted to the spot.

Seconds felt like hours as the three boys stood there, unmoving.

'Never turn the other cheek,' Tom remembered his father saying to him. 'Never. Always get your own back. 'Cos if you keep turning the other cheek, know what you get? Punch-drunk, that's what.'

Tom walked slowly towards Edward, fists raised. Edward, knowing what was coming was going to hurt, cowered away. He closed his eyes.

But the blow never came. Tom smiled instead and grabbed Edward. 'Let's play hide-and-seek,' he said, twisting the other boy's wrist, forcing him back into the room they had just left. 'You go first.'

He let go of Edward, and pushed him inside. Before Edward could run out again, Tom took hold of the door and pulled it shut. He felt Edward trying the handle, trying to pull it open, but Tom was too strong for him.

James stepped forward, opened his mouth as if about to speak, but the look in Tom's eyes silenced him. He stood there listening to the door being hit and kicked. Eventually there was silence.

Edward soon realised it was no good to keep pulling on the door handle. Tom had it held fast. He knew he couldn't open it until Tom let go. He gave up and walked back further into the room.

It suddenly felt colder, night-time cold. Edward could see his breath forming in misty clouds as he breathed out. He shivered, hugged himself.

There was something else about the room too. Something he didn't like. It wasn't just the cold and the dead birds in the fireplace, it was a sensation. A sadness. He was already feeling lost and desolate but this room seemed to be feeding on his sorrow, magnifying it. And there was something else: a sense of dread, of terror, moving towards him.

And then he noticed the wallpaper.

In the far corner, the old, damp paper began to crack and peel away from the wall. The black mould seemed to be getting even darker, starting to spread out from the corner.

Edward felt his heart jump into his mouth, his body begin to shake. He turned back to the door and hammered as hard as he could.

Tom laughed and held even harder on to the door handle. James just stood and watched. As mute as Edward.

✻

Edward turned away from the door, dared to glance back into the room once more. The mould was making its way round the walls towards him, like black wizened witch's fingers reaching slowly out, ready to clasp him, entrap him . . .

With renewed vigour, he began hammering again.

Eve was setting up her classroom in the dining room when she heard the noise. She immediately put down the books she had been laying out and ran to see what was happening.

Edward stopped hammering. He felt something touch him. He had never been so terrified in all his life.

He opened his mouth, let out a silent scream.

'What's going on?' Eve reached the nursery doorway.

Tom saw her coming and let go of the handle. He quickly moved away from the door.

'James made me do it,' he said weakly.

Eve ignored him and went straight to the door. She could hear Edward hammering on the other side. She tried the handle, but it wouldn't budge. She turned to Tom.

'Did you lock it?'

Tom shook his head. He realised he was in trouble now.

'Where's the key?' Eve shouted at him.

Tom kept shaking his head. 'I don't . . . We didn't . . .'

She advanced towards him. 'You must have unlocked it in the first place.'

'It . . . it was open . . .'

She towered over him, her eyes like two red-hot coals. 'Where is it?'

Tom cowered away from her, her anger making him too dumb to speak. She turned back to the door.

'Edward! Let me in!'

Eve twisted the handle, pushing and pulling at the door. Realising she was getting nowhere, she let go, curled her hands into fists and began frantically hammering on it. But still it wouldn't move.

Her knuckles sore, she turned to the other boys, ready to demand, once again, that they find the key. As she did so, the handle turned. The door swung slowly open of its own accord.

Seeing what was happening, Eve rushed inside, ready to grab Edward, fearing the worst. Then stopped. The boy was sitting on the floor in the middle of the room. In his hands was an old toy, and he was playing with it, seemingly contentedly.

Eve moved gingerly towards him. 'Edward?' she said quietly.

He didn't look up, just went on playing with his toy.

'Edward, are you all right?'

She got no response. It seemed as if he hadn't even heard her.

She knelt down beside him, gave him her hand. He took it, and as she straightened up he rose with her. She looked at what he was holding. It was an old Mr Punch puppet, his red tunic now mottled black, his gold braid hanging loose. Eve could still make out the features of his wooden face: eyes bright and blue, smile vivid, cheeks and hooked nose and pointed chin still red.

Edward allowed her to lead him out of the room, clutching Mr Punch tightly in his other hand.

As she left, Eve, frowning, noticed the state of the walls. The house seemed to be deteriorating by the hour. But she didn't have time to dwell on that.

She led Edward from the room, and closed the door firmly behind her.

A Visitor

Lunch was a sombre affair.

In the dining room, Tom and James were kept apart from the other children, going hungry. They sat at a separate table writing out lines as punishment, under Jean's watchful gaze.

I must not bully the other children.
I must not bully the other children.
I must not . . .

The others knew exactly what had happened and, just as they had regarded Edward the previous day, were studying the two transgressors with similar fascination.

Eve sat next to Edward. She was worried that his

experiences at the hands of Tom – and, she thought reluctantly, James – would have made him even more withdrawn. But the opposite seemed to have happened. He wasn't the boy he had been before he lost his mother, but he seemed, in his own mute way, to be unscathed by his ordeal.

However, he still wouldn't let go of Mr Punch.

'Where did you get that, Edward?' she asked him. There was something about the toy she didn't like. It made her uneasy, but she couldn't express why. It felt as if a small piece of that sad room had detached itself and latched on to Edward.

He didn't reply. Just finished his lunch, his focus all the time on the toy.

Eve continued. 'I saw some like that in the cellar. There was an old puppet theatre down there, too. Did you go down there to get it?'

He shook his head.

She leaned in closer, her voice dropping to conspiratorial level. 'You won't be in trouble if you did. I just want you to tell me how you came by it.'

Edward didn't respond. Encouraging him further, she placed her hand on his arm to comfort him. He briefly leaned into her, which she found reassuring, but he didn't let go of Mr Punch.

There was a knock at the front door.

'Get the door, please, Miss Parkins.'

Eve nodded and stood up. As she left the room she was aware of Jean, behind her, going to the window. Eve almost smiled. She wouldn't answer the door herself, but she wouldn't want to miss who was there.

What Eve didn't see was Edward. He waited until both the adults were otherwise distracted then crossed over to the table at which Tom and James were sitting. James looked anywhere but at his former friend.

Edward stood over Tom and handed him a note.

Give me back my drawing.

Tom put down his pencil, a nasty smile spanning his features. He shook his head.

Joyce saw what was happening and came over. She took in the note, along with Tom's reaction. 'Give it back,' she said, 'or I'll tell.'

Tom lunged forward, face an angry mask. 'I'll rip it.'

Joyce and Edward jumped back.

Eve knew nothing of this. She opened the front door, expecting Jim Rhodes, and found Harry instead. He was smiling, bundled inside his great-coat, rubbing his hands together in the cold.

'Thought I'd come and check up on you. See how you're getting on.' Then, quickly added, 'All of you, I mean.'

He saw a face at the window. Jean was watching him through the glass. 'Is this a bad time?'

Eve followed his gaze and Jean retreated. She smiled. 'No,' she said. 'Not at all.'

They both stood there, unmoving. He looked even more handsome in daylight, Eve thought, then chastised herself for thinking such a thing.

'Listen,' said Harry, 'I'm not a fan of pneumo-nia . . .'

Eve laughed and invited him in.

Psychic Powers

Not wanting Jean to accuse her of anything untoward, Eve continued her duties while talking to Harry. She was in the children's dormitory, making their beds. Harry was standing in front of a heater, still trying to get warm.

'Would you like a hand?' he asked.

Eve smiled. 'Thank you.'

He took off his greatcoat and joined her, tucking in, folding and pulling the sheets tight. 'Should be used to this by now,' he said.

'Indeed you should.'

Harry glanced at the door and dropped his voice. 'How's Sergeant Battleaxe?'

Eve looked round nervously. 'Be quiet, she'll hear. And it's Brigadier, not Sergeant. Well, wife of, anyway.'

Harry gave a mock shrug. 'I'm not scared.' He looked thoughtful. 'Although she does outrank me . . .'

Eve laughed, and it felt like the most relaxing thing she had done since she had left London.

Harry, smiling, picked up a book from a bedside table, looked at the cover. It was a romance novel, *I'll Be With You*, by Frances Braybrooke. He waved it at Eve. 'This hers? Bet it is. Tough on the outside, but deep down . . .' He shook his head.

Eve reddened slightly. 'Actually, it's mine. I left it in here by mistake.'

'Oh.' Harry carefully replaced it as if it were suddenly hot. He looked sheepish.

'Helps me take my mind off things,' she said, to make him feel better. 'Do you read?'

Harry shrugged. 'Manuals. You know, that kind of thing. Not too keen on stories.'

Eve smiled. 'Everyone likes stories.'

They had stopped working on the beds.

'So what's yours?' asked Harry.

Eve bent down, plumped up a pillow, avoiding his eyes. 'Thought you weren't keen,' she said.

Harry shrugged again. 'Try me.'

She stopped playing with the pillow, and gestured round the room. 'What about this house?' she said, deflecting his question. 'I'm sure there's an interesting story here.'

'Of rising damp, maybe.'

Eve bit her lip, her expression suddenly serious. 'I found a load of old things in the cellar last night.'

Harry laughed. 'Old things? In a cellar? Fancy that . . .'

Eve didn't smile. 'I think something bad happened here.'

Harry looked round. 'Well, the wallpaper's pretty ghastly . . .'

'I'm serious.' She threw a pillow at him. Surprised, he caught it. 'There's something about this place. It feels . . .' She thought of the old nursery, of Edward's newly discovered toy. 'Sad, or angry. Maybe both. I don't know . . .'

Harry rubbed his hands together, his eyes twinkling. 'Psychic powers, eh?' He crossed over to her and put the pillow down. 'Then tell me what I'm thinking . . .'

He gently placed two fingers on her brow. They were cool, but Eve enjoyed the touch. Hamming

it up, he made a show of acting like a stage mes-
merist, contorting his face as if in pain, waving his
other hand around. Then he mouthed a sentence at
her: 'Where are you from?'

Eve laughed. 'Croydon.'

He jumped back. 'Amazing! Again.' He replaced
his fingers on her brow, laughing. 'And now?' His
expression was slightly more serious. He didn't
mouth anything this time.

But Eve wasn't ready to be serious with him.
Not just yet. 'Do you want a cup of tea?' she asked,
smiling.

'Wrong answer.'

She thought some more. 'Oh, I don't know.
You'll have to tell me.'

'What's behind that smile?' he said, looking at
her thoughtfully.

Eve shook her head. 'Not that one again.'

'Like a broken record, me.' His laughter trailed
away and his fingers dropped.

Eve suddenly realised just how close he was to
her. His eyes were locked on to hers. 'It's just . . . my
way,' she said. 'How I cope.'

'With the war?' He seemed to have moved even
closer.

'With everything.'

She could feel his breath on her cheek, smell his aftershave. His eyes never left hers.

'Eve?'

She started, turned quickly. Jean was standing in the doorway. For how long, Eve had no idea.

Jean gave a brittle smile. 'I think it's time we had afternoon lessons, don't you?'

'Yes, of course,' said Eve, smoothing down the front of her dress, even though it wasn't creased.

Jean gave a curt nod. 'Good day, Captain.' She turned and left the room, stopping to ring the bell to summon the children.

Eve and Harry looked at each other and, the moment broken, laughed.

'I feel like one of her pupils,' said Harry. 'A naughty one.'

Eve laughed once more.

'Is that your work face again?' he asked.

She kept smiling, kept looking into his eyes.

'Perhaps this one's real,' she said.

Harry

The cold wind sent ripples through the water on either side of the Nine Lives Causeway. It built up into white peaks, lapped and landed at the sides of the road, fizzling away to nothing. Retracting, ready to encroach once more.

Harry's hands shook as he gripped hard on the wheel of his Jeep. He stared resolutely ahead as he drove, not allowing himself to be distracted by what was happening on either side of the vehicle. He hated the water. The sound of it built in his imagination. It was loud, almost deafening, a noise too great for the size of waves, amplified in his head until the rhythm of the waves became the rhythm of his breathing, his pulse. Roiling and crashing. Breath coming in increasingly ragged gasps, he couldn't cross the causeway quickly enough.

Then he heard something else on the wind, over and above the deafening sounds of the water. Faint and subtle, but unmistakable. A scream. Then another. A cry for help. Then nothing, the water claiming the voice, dragging it down.

Drowning it.

Harry stopped the Jeep and removed his shaking hands from the wheel. He tried to block out the sounds of the water, the echoing, fading screams that he still heard inside his head. He screwed his eyes tight shut, grimaced and, feeling the familiar impotence of rage and fear building within him once more, hit the steering wheel hard. Again and again, until, exhausted, he sat still, breathing heavily, trying to regain some kind of calm.

He rubbed his eyes, looked round. Listened. The drowning screams had disappeared. Harry wondered if he had actually heard them, or if they were just the screams he carried with him, inside his head.

He started the Jeep up once more, and drove for dry land as fast as he could.

Behind him, snow started to fall.

The Face Beneath the Floorboards

Eve shut the front door, turning the key firmly in the lock. Outside was cold, snow falling. Inside wasn't much warmer.

She was thinking of Harry's visit. She liked him. He was a charming, handsome young man. But she believed there was more to him than that. He seemed to carry something around with him, some melancholic air, some pain. He hid it well, and it wasn't visible to all. Only those who recognised something similar in themselves, Eve thought. A kindred spirit. And he seemed interested in her, too.

Smiling, she made her way down the hallway but came to an abrupt halt as a floorboard creaked beneath her foot. She placed her weight on it again. The board bent out of shape. It was black and rotten with a large hole in the centre. Dangerous, she thought, a job for Jim Rhodes when he came back. Or Harry. She smiled once more at the thought of him.

She knelt down to examine it. Then fell backwards in shock.

A pair of eyes. Shining with dark malevolence in a white face. Staring up at her through the floorboards.

Her heart racing, she knelt forward and looked through the hole.

There was no one there.

Eve stood up, looked round. There was no one else about. She headed to the kitchen and opened the door. And there was Jean sitting at the table, rubbing her ankles. She looked up as Eve entered.

'Kettle's just boiled,' she said, nodding to the cup of tea before her.

Eve stared at her. 'Were you just in the cellar?'

'A few minutes ago,' said Jean, finishing her ankle massage and sipping her tea. 'Not very pleasant, is it? Stinks to high heaven.'

Eve glanced at the door, then at Jean and the cup of tea in front of her, steam rising from it. Could it have been Jean she had seen through the floor-boards? Could she have made it back up in the time it took Eve to get from the hallway to the kitchen? And put the kettle on?

'Have some tea,' said Jean.

Eve snapped out of her trance. 'Tea. Yes. Tea.'

Is something happening to me? thought Eve. *Am I going mad? Last night and now this?* She took a cup down from the cupboard, poured herself some tea from the pot.

A hallucination, she thought. *That's what it was. Like last night. Yes. A hallucination.*

She sat down at the table with her tea. *Don't think about it*, she told herself, *talk about something else.*

'Was . . . your husband called up when the war started?' Eve asked, then immediately regretted it. Eve knew from experience that Jean didn't take kindly to questions about her personal life.

But to Eve's surprise, Jean smiled. 'No,' she

said. 'We've been in the services our whole lives. Our two boys, too.'

Eve leaned forward, responding to this new-found warmth. 'Do you have any photos?'

The shutters came back down. 'I know what they look like.'

Eve put the cup to her lips, took a drink and, refreshed, tried again. 'Where are they?' she asked, quietly.

Jean took a sip of tea. As she swallowed the liquid, she seemed to relax a little more. 'One's in Africa, the other in France. My husband is in France, too.' She looked away from Eve, took another mouthful.

'Do you . . .'

Jean turned back to her. 'I try not to think about them. They're not here. If I started wondering, then . . . who knows where my mind would lead me?'

She looked away once more, but Eve had seen the glitter in the corners of Jean's eyes. She thought again of Jim Rhodes's words and didn't press her further.

Jean drained her cup, stood up. 'Goodnight, Eve.'

Eve's mouth fell open. That was the first time her headmistress had called her by her first name.

She was so startled, she could barely say goodnight in reply.

Fire in the Sky

Edward couldn't sleep. He had closed his eyes tight, and lay as unmoving as he could in his bed, but it was no good. He was still awake, his thumb firmly in his mouth, Mr Punch clutched close to his chest. He knew the rest of the children were talking about him, and while it didn't help, that wasn't the only thing keeping him awake.

He heard Tom tell Fraser that he thought Edward had seen a ghost when he was locked in the nursery. This excited Fraser, who was so full of questions and wild speculation that Edward, listening to it, knew he would never get any sleep tonight.

He sat up, put his glasses on and looked round

the dormitory. A few candles were still burning, the only illumination in the room. Tom and Fraser were lying in their adjacent beds, whispering to each other. They saw Edward was awake. Fraser stared at him, open-mouthed. Tom just looked straight at him.

'Didn't you?' Tom said, knowing Edward had heard everything they had said. 'You saw a ghost, didn't you, Edward?'

Edward made no reply.

'Was it your mummy?' asked Fraser, and Flora, listening in, winced at the small boy's insensitivity.

'Leave him alone,' she said.

Tom turned on her. 'Say what I like. He's not your boyfriend, is he?'

'Be quiet.' Joyce spoke in her usual schoolteacher-in-training voice. 'I shall tell Mrs Hogg about this. About all of you.'

Alfie pulled the blankets over his head, and curled himself up. 'I just want to go to sleep,' he said, his voice muffled and tired.

Edward turned away from all of them and put his hands over his ears. He had to block them out. Block everything out.

He stared at the wall.

And a hideous face appeared right in front of him.

Edward jerked back, panicked and fell out of bed. He risked looking up at the grotesque face, flinching, hiding his eyes with his fingers in case it was going to scare him again. He saw it for what it really was. Tom wearing his gas mask.

'Got you,' the boy said, taking it off and throwing it aside. Laughing, he walked back to his bed.

Edward pulled himself slowly up off the floor and, ashamed and embarrassed, climbed back into bed. He clutched Mr Punch even tighter.

Tom was clearly enjoying the anguish he had caused Edward, but it wasn't enough. He knew that the rest of the children's sympathies didn't lie with him, but he was still determined to provoke more of a reaction.

Tom held up Edward's drawing and waved it at him. Then he made a show of folding it up, putting it in his pyjama pocket, patting it. Edward felt distressed beyond words.

'Give it back.'

The whole group sat up to see what was happening. James was standing at the foot of Tom's bed, hands on hips.

'I said, give it back to Edward.'

Tom stared at him in amazement. This was the first time James had stood up to him. The first time anyone in the group had done so. And from the look on James's face, he wasn't going to back down. Not without a fight.

Tom threw back his bedclothes and squared up to him. But the fight didn't get started, because at that moment, outside the window, they heard a rumbling drone. They knew immediately what it was. Months of air raids on London had told them that.

The fight forgotten, they all got out of their beds and rushed over to the windows, jostling each other for the clearest view, cupping their eyes to see better.

In the distance, out in the winter sky above the sea, was a squadron of Halifax bombers making its way home.

'It's a raid!' screamed Fraser.

'They're English, idiot,' said Alfie.

The little boy looked round, embarrassed. 'I knew that,' he said.

Joyce shushed them, pointed. 'Look.'

One of the bombers was on fire. It started to

fall away from the rest of the group. The children all stared, enrapt, whispering prayers, words of encouragement, willing it to stay aloft.

None of them noticed as, behind the candles' pale and flickering light, one shadow detached itself from the rest and moved towards the children. Dressed in black, her face bleached-bone white, she came and stood behind them. While they looked at the plane, she looked at them, her coal-black eyes dancing with undisguised malevolence. Looking along the line, choosing . . .

'What on earth is going on here?'

Jean stood in the doorway, about to admonish the children further, but when she saw what they were looking at, came to join them.

Unseen, the dark figure with the bleached-bone face receded into the shadows.

In the sky, the plane could no longer keep up. The fire had spread all along its fuselage and consumed one wing. It began to fall, flames enveloping it even further. They all watched as it spiralled down into the sea. When it hit the surface of the water, it was so far away it barely made a sound.

The rest of the squadron passed over and the night was quiet again. The sea calm now, as if nothing had ever disturbed its surface. But they were all still staring, looking at the empty sky, trying to take in what they had just seen. Even Jean.

In her room, Eve had also watched it happen. But she had closed her eyes before the plane hit the water. She clutched the cherub pendant tight to her throat.

'Please let it not be Harry . . .'

Another Presence

His mother was smiling and she was wearing her best coat. The black one. She was calling to him, and Edward, his heart bursting with joy to see her again, was running as fast as he could towards her.

Everything had been a dream, he thought as he ran. The air raid, the explosion, the house, the nursery . . . everything. This was real. This was happening.

He kept running, almost reaching her, almost there. But every time he came close to her, she seemed to move further away. Always distant, always out of touch, calling to him but knowing he could never reach her. Then at last he began to make some headway. He could have cried out in joy, laughed aloud. He was going to hold his mother again. Soon. Now.

Only it wasn't his mother any more. She had changed. She was still wearing black but it wasn't his mother's good coat. Her clothes were old, shabby. And she wore something over her face — a veil? It didn't hide the face beneath. He could see her white skin stretched tight so it looked like dead, weathered bone; her eyes, black and hard, glittering with spite and malice. And he was running towards her.

He tried to make himself stop, force his feet to slow down, but his pace only increased, his legs pumping faster. He shook his head, tried to cry out, but his voice wouldn't work. *This is the dream*, he thought. *Not before. Please let me wake up, please. . .*

Edward sat bolt upright, his chest bursting from dream-exertion, sweat on his brow. He opened his eyes. The room was in darkness, the candles having long burned down. Everything was a blur as he hadn't yet put his glasses on, but he could see enough to know that the others were sound asleep.

He reached for his glasses on the bedside table but in doing so knocked them to the floor. Leaning out of bed, he groped around but couldn't seem to reach them. Behind him he heard the sound of something cracking, shifting. Crumbling.

He sat up, looked round. The only thing behind him was the wall. Was the wall cracking? He squinted, tried to see. All he could make out were vague shapes moving against the shadows.

Then one of the shadows began to make its way towards him. As it did so, the sound of cracking was replaced by another sound. Slithering, susurrating. The shadow was moving fast, becoming bigger and bigger, looming towards him. There was an awful stench of decay and rot. It made him feel instantly nauseous.

Terrified, he pulled the blankets over his head and lay down as quickly as he could. Mr Punch was under the covers with him, and he pulled the puppet against his chest, felt his hard, wooden nose and cheek push into him.

He held tight to the blanket, not daring to move, barely breathing, willing himself to be weightless and invisible. Tried to do what his mother used to tell him, think good thoughts to drive the bad dreams away. Hoped that it would work on whatever or whoever was there.

Then something tried to pull the blanket off him.

Edward gripped it, as hard as he could, but the presence fought back. Determined not to give in, Edward used all of his strength just to hold on.

The blanket went slack in Edward's hands. He heard the slithering and rustling noise again, retreating this time. The awful smell began to dissipate. He stayed still, listening. Eventually, he heard nothing but his own breathing.

Edward trembled, forced back his cries in case the shadow heard him. He kept his eyes tight shut, willed himself to fall asleep once more, go back to his dream. The good part, with his mother. One hand clutched Mr Punch to his chest; the fingers of the other were stuffed in his mouth to stifle any screams.

He lay like that for the rest of the night

The woman with the bleached-bone face turned away from the foetal Edward and scanned the dormitory, settling her attention on Tom. As she did so, the atmosphere in the room changed, crackling now with a palpable malice.

Tom sat up in bed and blinked. Once. Twice.

His eyes were open but his expression was blank. He threw the covers back, got out of bed. Still in his pyjamas and with bare feet, he made his way out of the room.

He reached the front door, waited. The door swung slowly open for him.

Outside, the snow was still falling. The wind blew flurries through the door, the cold flakes hitting Tom's face like icy needles. He didn't flinch, didn't even blink, but turned away from the snow, ready to move back inside the house.

The woman stood behind him, preventing his return. He paused and looked at her, nodded. He understood. Then, barefoot, he stepped out into the freezing cold night.

The door gently closing behind him.

Discovery

Edward was exhausted. He didn't feel like he had been asleep, but he had, and judging from all the activity in the room around him, he was the last one awake.

He found his glasses on the floor, put them on. His two teachers were moving round the room, checking under beds, in cupboards, turning to each other and shaking their heads. He could sense their tension. The rest of the children were up and moving about too, their expressions grim. Realising that something serious was going on, Edward decided he had better get up and join them.

As he did so, he noticed something poking out

from underneath his pillow. He pulled it out. It was the drawing Tom had stolen from him. The woman and the boy. He looked round, hoping to see who had put it there. James, probably, or Joyce. But no one acknowledged him finding it. No one acknowledged him at all.

He looked round again. Where was Tom?

In the hallway, Jean walked towards the front door and turned the handle. It opened.

She gave an accusatory stare at Eve, who was standing behind her. Eve's eyes widened in shock.

'But I locked it . . .'

She hurried over to join Jean at the door. Around the handle and the lock the wood was dark and discoloured, rot and decay setting in. She was aware that all the children had left the dormitory and were watching them. 'Everybody, please stay inside,' she said as she and Jean went to get their coats.

They still wore their nightgowns underneath, and Eve felt the cold on her legs and hands. The ground was covered in icy, slushy snow.

Eve began searching in front of the house. She could see the causeway stretching across to the mainland, the water becalmed for now. She looked down at the ground and saw footprints leading away from the front door. They led to the barbed wire on the edge of the island.

She ran towards it. Saw something tangled up in it. Tom.

His body was twisted, caught at an unnatural angle, as if he had been determined to push himself through and escape, but the razor-sharp coils had caught him and held him back. His lips were blue. The blood from the barbed-wire cuts and slashes had formed on his body as ruby-red teardrops of ice.

He had frozen to death.

Aftermath

Eve looked at the seven small faces staring up at her, their features full of shock and sadness. They wanted answers, explanations and reassurance, but Eve had none to give. *Explaining the war is easy compared to this*, she thought, *because I don't understand myself what's happened.*

Jean and Eve had gathered the children in their dormitory. Jean had started talking to them, trying to explain what had happened to Tom. It was a long, rambling speech, with very little of her usual clipped, no-nonsense tones. Eve thought she seemed to be struggling to find answers herself and that if she kept talking long enough, those answers would come to her.

'I know you've all . . . all lost someone or know of someone who has lost someone in the Blitz . . .' She struggled to keep her attention away from Edward, not to single the boy out. 'And . . . and . . . you get used to it. But you shouldn't have to . . . you shouldn't have to, it's . . .' She turned away from them, took a few seconds, composed herself. 'This, this is different. Here, in this house, on this island, is different, but just as dangerous.' Another deep breath. She cleared her throat, smoothed down the front of her unwrinkled blouse. 'Last night was a . . . a terrible accident. Terrible . . . And you must understand that, that . . . out in the countryside, here, there is still danger.'

Out of the corner of her eye Eve noticed a patch of mould on the wall behind Tom's bed. It seemed to be moving, pulsating. Growing. She looked at it full on. No, it wasn't moving, but she was certain it hadn't been there before.

Jean was still talking. 'You must . . . must obey the rules. Yes. Obey the rules. That's . . . that's how we survive. That's how we . . . get through things. Yes. Obey the rules. I . . . I cannot stress that enough.'

There was an abrupt clatter from the hallway. The children, jumpy now, all turned to see what it was. The front door had been thrown back and Jim Rhodes was carrying Tom's blanket-wrapped body through the house, ready to take him off the island.

A morbid excitement rippled through the group. The children were caught between obeying their teacher and the illicit thrill of wanting to see their dead friend.

Jean marched over to the door, closing it tight. She turned back to the children.

'I want everyone to . . . to stay inside today. Even . . . even at playtime.' She closed her eyes, shook her head, then looked up once more, turning to Eve. 'Miss Parkins, see that Dr Rhodes has everything he needs. I . . . I'm going to write to the boy's mother.'

Jean was straight through the door, banging it shut behind her. Her composure was dissolving, and she couldn't allow the children to witness that. But Eve had seen her shoulders shake and the tears start to fall before the door closed.

Eve turned to the children. And found she had nothing to say.

She gave them what she hoped was a reassuring smile and went to find Jim Rhodes.

✻

The barbed wire had been cut and rolled back to allow Tom's body to be removed. It had then been twisted back into place, covering up the resulting hole. Now, the only thing that marked the location was the remaining blood.

Jim Rhodes was outside standing by his bus, surveying the estate, wrapped up in a thick coat and scarf, trying not to let his eyes settle on the spot where Tom's body had been found, but he couldn't stop his focus being drawn back to there.

Eve came out and stood alongside him. For a moment, neither of them spoke. Their breath forming cold plumes, ghosting away into nothing.

'I . . . I was sure I locked it,' she said eventually. 'The front door. Sure of it.'

Jim Rhodes shook his head, his eyes averted from hers. 'I did say you had to be careful.'

'I know, and I . . .' Eve sighed. 'I'm sorry.'

Jim turned to face her. 'I don't think any of us could ever be sorry enough.'

Eve looked away. Her eyes alighted on the repaired hole in the barbed-wire fence. She shuddered. The drying blood had taken on the colour of rust. It looked to Eve like an external echo of the spreading mould inside the house. She turned back to Jim Rhodes.

'Doctor,' she said. Her voice was hesitant, but her emotion heartfelt. 'There's something wrong here.'

Jim Rhodes frowned. 'What d'you mean?'

Eve looked back at the house and lowered her voice, as if its presence would inhibit what she was about to say. 'There's the walls . . . black marks all over them, mould. And it's spreading when you, when you don't look at it . . . it was on the . . . the door this morning, the front door . . . and it wasn't there last night . . .'

Jim Rhodes said nothing.

Eve couldn't stop. All her fears were pouring out of her. 'And . . . the face. I . . . I saw a face. Through the floorboards. The cellar. In the cellar. A white face. And I heard sounds, like . . . like . . .' She closed her eyes, tried to force herself to remember. 'Backwards and forwards . . . And no one else heard it . . . And . . . and there was writing . . .'

She stopped talking, the fear she had kept contained inside her exhausting itself.

'I know it . . . it sounds silly, especially in daylight, but . . .' She sighed. 'We need to get out of here. All of us.'

Jim Rhodes's eyes were filled with compassion as he spoke. 'I told you, there's nowhere else to go.' He took her hand in his, his compassion now tempered by worry. 'Look,' he said, holding her hand tight, his voice measured, like he was giving a grave diagnosis to a patient. 'I think it might be best if you leave when the new staff arrive.'

Eve was shocked. This wasn't the response she had expected at all. She stepped back, her hand falling from his. 'No, no . . . I'm not making this up . . . I didn't . . .'

Jim Rhodes continued. 'We shouldn't have expected you to be ready for this kind of full-time care. You're only young.'

Eve had a sudden image of herself as a tragic heroine in a Victorian novel, denounced as hysterical, her complaints not believed, and about to be committed to an asylum for her own good. 'No,' she said, 'this has got nothing to do with . . . I am ready. I promise.'

The empathy in Jim Rhodes's eyes verged on the painful. He took her hand once more. 'The new staff will be better suited to this. It's nothing personal. But they're all parents themselves.' He patted her hand, gave her what he felt was a reassuring smile. 'I'm sure you understand.'

Eve couldn't find the words to respond. She turned, and realised that Edward was standing on the front steps. He must have heard every word.

The boy stared at her, his expression unreadable. He held up the puppet. Its red, wooden face seemed to be leering at her, mocking her.

Edward turned and went back inside.

The Angel of Death

All around, the snow was melting. The ice crust was thin and brittle, and Eve's shoes shattered it easily, sinking to the soft, wet grass and earth beneath. One fragile world shattering to reveal another.

The children were inside the house. Eve would have said they were safe there, except she was starting to believe that might not be the case. At least they were all together and Jean was looking after them, so Eve didn't have to worry too much about them.

She walked through the mist-wrapped woods, not noticing which direction she had come from, not caring which direction she was headed in. She hadn't been able to stay near the house, had to get away. Jim Rhodes's words still echoed round her head, guilt and grief intermingling.

She stopped walking, touched the cherub pendant round her neck and closed her eyes.

She wanted to cry, to scream, to be somewhere else. Someone else. She felt tears prick the corners of her closed eyes, fought them back. She wouldn't give in, she couldn't give in . . .

She opened her eyes again, wiping the tears away. Through the trees ahead of her, silhouetted against the mist, was an indistinct figure. Eve moved to the side of a tree to get a better look. Then slowly walked towards the figure.

A woman, dressed all in black. But not contemporary clothes; these were decades old. She wore a black veil, but even from a distance Eve could make out her bleached-bone skin, her dark, glittering eyes. Shock coursed through Eve's body. She recognised the face as the one she had seen through the floorboards in the cellar. The woman glared at Eve.

'What are you doing here?' Eve called to her. 'What do you want?'

The woman just turned and slowly walked away.

'Wait . . .'

Eve began to hurry after her, but the woman kept moving away. She disappeared behind a clutch of trees and Eve sped up, not wanting to lose her. But the woman always seemed to be ahead of her. No matter how fast Eve ran, she couldn't reach her. It felt like she had slipped into a dream, a realm where waking logic no longer applied.

'Come back . . .'

Eve ran even faster. So intent had she been on catching up with the retreating figure that she hadn't taken notice of her surroundings. She had long since left the path and was now on a higher ridge with a steep slope down on her left. Melting snow covered the unfamiliar terrain and she misjudged a step, causing her to lose her balance. She slipped and fell, rolling down the hill.

She went through bracken and brambles, mud, slush and ice, until she came to rest at the bottom of the hill, her back against something cold and hard, the air knocked out of her. She kept her eyes closed until she regained her breath, then opened them.

And screamed.

A figure loomed above her, arms outstretched,

wings unfolded. Heart pounding, she realised that she was looking up at a statue of an angel.

Eve slowly got to her feet, brushing the mud from her clothes. She was in a graveyard. She scanned the surrounding area. The woman she had been chasing was nowhere to be seen.

The gravestones caught her attention. They were all old, as old as the house, she presumed. An attempt had been made to smarten them up – probably for the children's arrival – but it was only cosmetic and largely futile. They were in bad repair. Decaying away to nothing, like the bodies beneath them had done. She could just make out the inscription on the nearest one:

NATHANIEL DRABLOW

August 2nd 1863 – December 29th 1871

8 years of age.

Beloved son of

Alice and Charles Drablow

Someone, Eve noticed, had attempted to scratch out the final sentence. Eve examined another stone.

JENNET HUMFRYE

Eve couldn't read any more on that one. The stone had a huge crack across the front of it. It looked like it had either been split by lightning or someone had tampered with it.

Eve straightened up and shivered. Graveyards didn't usually scare her. After all, there was nothing to fear from the dead, she always rationalised, only the living. But she didn't like it here. She felt very uneasy.

Turning round, she hurried back to the house. She didn't look back.

Spilt Milk

James didn't like his milk. It tasted different from what he was used to in London; thicker and warmer. Mrs Hogg had told them that they were lucky to have it, that the milk in the country was so much fresher than that in the city. Even so, thought James, he still preferred London milk. He preferred London everything.

The children were all sitting round the dining table eating lunch. No one had spoken while they were eating; in fact they hadn't even looked at each other. James was thinking about Tom. He kept thinking of when they would play cowboys and Indians, or Nazis and commandos, when one of them would get shot, die and then get up again, ready to fire back against their enemy. But Tom wouldn't be getting up again. Ever.

He had seen Miss Parkins come in covered in mud, and go upstairs to change. She had been in a hurry, hoping no one had seen her. James wouldn't tell. He prided himself that he wasn't like that. He did wonder where she had been, though. Perhaps she had had her own bad experience with the barbed wire. He shook his head and tried not to think about it. Miss Parkins had come down and joined them, but she looked as upset as the rest of them. She was hardly eating, either. He took another mouthful of milk, then remembered he didn't like it.

Edward was sitting opposite him. He hadn't touched his food. He just stared at his precious drawing in his lap, that tatty old Mr Punch puppet never far from him. James wished he could do something to help him. Everything he had said or done since they had arrived had turned out to be the wrong thing. He desperately wanted a way to make things up to his friend. Make him happy again.

'Can I have your roll?'

Alfie, sitting next to Edward, had cleared his

plate but was still hungry. He was looking at Edward, seeking permission to start on his next.

Edward didn't even acknowledge the question. Alfie took Edward's silence as an affirmative and reached over to Edward's plate, ready to take the bread. James pushed Alfie's hand away. Alfie looked up, startled.

'He didn't say yes,' said James. 'You can't just take it.'

Alfie was surprised by James's outburst but not put off. He shrugged and reached out again for the roll. James grabbed his hand this time, determined not to let him get it, upset with himself for not standing up for Edward earlier, desperate to make up for it now.

But as he did so, James accidentally knocked over his glass of milk. It fell sideways, the milk spilling out all over Edward's lap.

Jean, alert as ever, was on her feet. 'Careful, James . . .'

Both teachers came over to the table.

Edward moved the drawing out of the way, but he wasn't quick enough. The milk had already hit it, wetting the paper, smudging the drawing. He looked at James, his eyes brimming with hurt.

Eve began to mop up the mess with a napkin. As she did so, James looked at Edward, his expression apologetic.

'I didn't mean to do it,' James said. 'I'm sorry, it was an accident . . .'

But Edward didn't hear him. He was on his feet, launching himself at James, kicking and punching, furious with him. James was so surprised he barely had time to bring up his hands to defend himself.

Eve was right beside them. She dropped the napkin and put her arms round Edward, grabbing him hard from behind, shouting at him to stop it, trying to pull him away from James.

Edward didn't respond. Tears in his eyes, he just kept pummelling away. Eve tried to turn his face round.

'Look at me . . . Edward, please, look at me . . .'

He just shrugged her away. She kept her arms tightly encircling him, not letting him move, and gradually his temper subsided. James stood away from him, body tensed, fists clenched in adrenalin-charged silence.

Miss Parkins looked at Edward's drawing. She saw what it was – a woman and a boy – and immediately understood why it would be so precious to

Edward. James also knew how much it meant to Edward, but he was so angry that he didn't care.

I tried to be nice, James thought, *tried to stand up for him, and this is the thanks I get. Well, I've had it with him . . .*

There was a knock at the door.

'Hello there,' said a cheerful voice, 'the door was open so I . . .'

Harry, the RAF captain, stepped into the room. His smile froze as he saw the collection of frightened, angry and grief-stricken faces.

'Oh,' he said, 'have I picked a bad time?'

Faith and Belief

Eve was bundled up in her heavy coat and scarf. Beside her, Harry had his greatcoat wrapped firmly round him. They made their way along the shoreline at the back of the house, the shingle gravelly, hard and snow-crusted beneath her shoes. The pair of them walked apart. The tide had gone out, leaving an expanse of black and grey mud beyond the stones. Knowing the causeway was open should have made Eve feel more connected to the mainland, less isolated. But seeing how desolate and treacherous her surroundings looked made her feel even more alone. The sky was empty, the only clouds their misting breath.

After Harry's sudden appearance, Jean had decided Eve should get some fresh air, put some distance between herself and the recent events in the house. 'Go for a walk,' she'd said, and Eve didn't need to be told twice. Since telling Harry what had happened, there had been silence. But the further they walked from the house, the more those words felt to Eve like a confessional and she now felt long-dammed tears welling in her eyes. She wiped them away, attempted a smile to cover her sadness.

'Sorry . . .'

'You've no need to be sorry,' said Harry, concern in his eyes. 'What happened wasn't your fault.'

She nodded absently, as if agreeing to something she hadn't heard correctly. They walked on in silence again. Eventually, Eve spoke.

'We brought them here to get away from all that.'

'All what?' he asked.

'The war, fighting, death . . .' She turned her head away from him, spoke into the wind. 'Safer in the country?' She shook her head. 'Oh, I don't know, perhaps I didn't lock it after all. I could have been distracted, I . . .' She sighed. 'Maybe I forgot.'

'Don't blame yourself. He could have unlocked the door himself.'

'But I had the key.'

Harry held up a finger. '*A* key. I doubt there'll just be one, house of that size. He could have, I don't know, found one of them lying round in another room, perhaps.'

'Or someone gave it to him.'

'There you go,' said Harry. 'Could have been one of the other children.'

'No,' said Eve firmly, 'not one of the children.'

Harry frowned. 'Who, then?'

Eve looked away, her eyes on the water but not seeing it. Instead she saw a white face with staring, rage-filled eyes.

'I think . . . I think there's someone else on this island.'

'What, you mean living here?'

Eve nodded. 'I heard someone in the cellar the night we arrived. I went down to investigate, but they had gone. Then this morning there was . . . I saw someone by the graveyard.'

'Did you talk to them?'

'I tried, but she . . . she disappeared.'

'Disappeared,' said Harry.

'Yes. Anyway, perhaps this . . . this woman unlocked the door last night.'

Harry nodded but didn't reply. Eve felt foolish for having told him about the woman. She realised how unconvincing her words must sound to him. So unconvincing that she now didn't dare tell him about the face under the floorboards.

Harry stopped walking, and placed his hands on Eve's shoulders. She stared up at him, expecting to be told that she was imagining things, that it was all in her head. Well-meaning but patronising words.

'Maybe we should take a look around,' Harry said, 'ask if anyone else has seen her.'

Eve blinked, wide-eyed. 'You mean, you believe me? You believe what I've just told you?'

Harry gave a puzzled smile. 'Why wouldn't I?'

Eve returned his smile, honest and unforced. Despite everything that had happened, this was the most positive she had felt since she had arrived at the house.

Harry had faith in her. She could have cried once more.

The first person they needed to talk to, Eve decided, was Edward. The boy hadn't been the same since he had emerged from the locked room. Eve sensed that he had seen something – or someone – that could help them, or at least validate what Eve had experienced.

Edward sat at the bottom of the staircase, notebook in hand, Eve and Harry kneeling down beside him.

Eve smiled at him. 'Look, Edward,' she said, 'you're not in trouble. I just need to talk to you, that's all. Is that all right?'

Edward gave a wary nod.

Eve smiled all the brighter. 'Good,' she said. 'Right, Edward. We need to know what happened when the boys locked you in that room. Can you tell us what happened?'

Edward looked away, shook his head.

Eve and Harry exchanged a glance. Eve found encouragement in Harry's eyes. She continued. 'Did you see something?'

Edward's eyes darted left and right like a trapped animal looking for an escape route.

Eve carried on, calm but insistent. 'Did you? Did you see something?'

Eventually Edward nodded.

Eve smiled once more. 'Good,' she said. 'What did you see?'

Edward gave no response, just clutched tightly

to the creepy old Mr Punch puppet. Eve noticed the paint had started to peel off the wood, giving its face a dissolute and corrupted aspect. Edward's hand was trembling.

'You can write it down,' she said.

Edward thought for a moment, took out his pencil, then passed the notebook to Eve.

She told me not to tell.

Eve felt her heart skip slightly at the words. She wasn't imagining things. She leaned forward.

'Who? Who told you not to?'

Edward shook his head, brow furrowed.

'Please, Edward, it's very important that you tell us . . .'

He shook his head once more, more firmly this time. Eve took his hands in hers. They were frozen.

'You mustn't listen to her,' Eve said. 'Do you hear me? Whatever she says. You mustn't listen to her.'

Edward pulled his hands away from her, his head dropping.

'Please, Edward,' said Eve, desperation and hurt in her voice now. 'I thought we were friends . . .'

Edward looked up and what Eve saw in his eyes almost broke her heart. Tears were forming and welling, his face creased with pain.

Eve sighed. 'I'm sorry, Edward. You can . . . go. Just . . . go now.'

He ran away from her as fast as he could, back to the dormitory, clutching the puppet tightly to him.

She turned to Harry. 'I've lost him,' she said. 'I thought I was so close to him, but . . .' She shook her head. 'Now what do we do?'

Eve stared at the dropped notebook, the one sentence staring up at her.

She told me not to tell.

Faith and Action

'It wasn't as bad as this before . . .'

The whole of the cellar floor was submerged in water. Eve could feel it seeping into her shoes, and the stench of rot was even worse.

'Must be a leak somewhere,' said Harry, looking around. 'But it doesn't seem as if anybody's living down here . . .'

Eve felt something nudge her ankle, and gasped in shock. Harry was right there at her side.

'What is it?' she said, eyes closed, not daring to look.

Harry straightened up, held out something long, grey and slithery in his hand. 'An eel,' he said, 'a dead one. Don't know how that got in . . .'

'Get rid of it,' she said, head averted. 'Please. I can't stand those things. And it stinks. But then this whole place does . . .'

Harry threw the eel away in the corner, wiping his hands on the stone wall. 'Thought you'd like those things,' he said, smiling. 'You know, being a Londoner and that. Jellied, isn't it?'

Eve grimaced. 'Please.'

They began to search the cellar, going through box after rotten box, pulling out papers and letters, all damp and mildewed, age-faded and decayed. Some crumbled and disintegrated when touched. They soon realised there was nothing that could help them with the present; only fragments of the past.

While Harry was absorbed with one box, taking out papers, studying them, shaking his head and replacing them, Eve watched him.

'Was that you,' she said, 'last night?'

He turned to her, frowning.

'Flying over the sea. A squadron of Halifaxes?'

'Oh,' he said, 'right.' He shook his head. She couldn't see his eyes when he answered. 'No. Not my turn, I'm afraid.'

She was about to ask him further questions, but he had spotted the phonograph. 'Hey,' he said, smiling, 'haven't seen one of those since I was a boy . . .'

'It doesn't work,' said Eve. 'I've tried it.'

He picked it up off the shelf and began running his fingers over it, examining it. 'You leave that to me.'

Seeing he was engrossed in it, Eve went back to scouring the box nearest to her. She found something solid inside. Bringing it out, she held it up to the weak light, examined it. A key, and written on the side were two initials: HJ.

She scanned the cellar, looking for a suitable lock to try it on but couldn't find anything. As she did so, a bell rang upstairs.

'That's the bell for the end of break. I'd better . . .'

Harry nodded, looked back at the phonograph. 'Off you go, then. I'll see if I can fix this.'

She smiled. 'Thank you.'

And ran up the stairs.

'Right, children,' she said once she had reached the makeshift classroom, 'this afternoon, I want you all to write a story about' — her eyes roved round the room, looking for inspiration — 'this house. Yes. This house. Whatever comes to mind.'

The children were all looking at her quizzically. She knew they were wondering why her feet were wet, but none of them had dared to ask her and she hadn't volunteered the information.

Eve tried not to look at Edward, to see what his reaction was. The exercise was for his benefit. She wanted to see what he would come up with.

Joyce put her hand up.

'Yes, Joyce.'

'Isn't it our times tables now?'

'Well, normally, yes, it would be. But not today.' She stood up, walked to the door, gripping the newly discovered key firmly. 'We'll do those later. I just have to pop out. I'll be back soon.'

'But you can't leave us,' said Joyce, voice indignant.

Eve stopped at the door, thought.

'Joyce,' she said, 'I'm leaving you in charge while I'm gone. It's a big responsibility, so make sure everyone gets on with their work.'

Joyce, as Eve had expected, couldn't have looked more proud.

✳

While they were busy working, Eve went through the house, key in hand. She tried doors, cabinets, drawers, anything with a keyhole, no matter how big or small. Eventually she had exhausted all the locks she could think of, but hadn't found a single one that it fitted.

She went to see how Harry was getting on.

Ghosts of the Past

Harry had carried the phonograph out of the cellar, laying it on the kitchen table. This room was easier to work in, and drier, plus – and he didn't normally hold with all that supernatural nonsense – something about that cellar unnerved him. More than just the smell, it was . . . he didn't know. He couldn't explain. His was a practical vocabulary not given to flights of fancy, but there was definitely something not right about the place.

The repair was proving trickier than he had expected. Harry was normally good with his hands, but bringing life back to this old, rusted, decayed piece of equipment seemed to be beyond him. He realigned the cylinder shaft one last time and gave the hand crank another turn.

'Right,' he said, wiping the dirt and rust off his fingers. 'Come on, you little . . .'

The machine whirred into life.

'Got you . . .' Harry couldn't keep the delight from his voice. He plugged in the rope-cord headphones and placed them over his ears. The sound he could hear was warped, scratched. Indistinct and distorted. A woman's voice came through in snatches and crackles. Distant and hesitant. A ghost from the past.

'. . . Alice Drablow . . .' The next sentence was lost. '. . . Marsh House my whole life . . .'

Got that, thought Harry, mentally filling in the missing words. He waited, but there was nothing more. He moved the needle forward along the cylinder. Through the hiss of static the voice emerged again.

'Nathaniel's drowned and she blames me . . .' More static. '. . . a better mother than she could ever have . . .'

He moved the needle around, placing it on different sections of the cylinder, trying to get Alice Drablow's voice back, but to no avail. That segment had completely deteriorated. With a sigh of exasperation, Harry moved on to a point where the static was low. But all he could hear was ambient silence. He was about to give up when a new voice came through, faint and distant.

'Never forgive. Never forget.'

Then silence. Harry leaned forward, listening hard, willing the voice to speak again. It returned, louder this time, closer. Like the speaker was right beside him, whispering in his ear. He could almost feel the breath on his neck.

'Never forgive. Never forget.'

Harry shivered.

Behind him, through the open door leading down to the cellar, a shadow appeared on the wall, swelling and looming as it came up the stairs. Harry, his concentration entirely taken with the phonograph, began to feel uneasy as Alice's voice returned.

'Jennet, I'm . . .' The crackling took over. '. . . sister . . .'

Even in the bad state the recording was in, there was no mistaking the fear in Alice Drablow's voice. Her voice shook as she spoke.

Behind Harry, the shadow on the wall became

elongated as the figure reached the entrance at the top of the cellar stairs. Harry felt a tightening in his chest, his breathing becoming laboured. *No*, he thought, *not now, not here . . .*

Alice's voice continued.

'Get . . .' More hissing. '. . . from me. You're not . . .' The recording skipped forward. Harry couldn't bring it back. '. . . imagining you. You're . . .' More static. '. . . guilty conscience . . .' Crackling. '. . . I said, get away from me!'

The last sentence was screamed out, then nothing more. Just the whir and wheeze of the ancient machine, the sound of Alice Drablow's strenuous breathing from years before.

The shadow stretched right round the room, reaching out along the wall and over the ceiling, down towards Harry. He felt the pain in his chest increase and a black, watery darkness engulf him. Other voices came to him then, ones not on the recording.

'*Help me . . . help me, Captain . . .*'

He closed his eyes. Suddenly there came an awful, distorted shriek. He cried out, the sound assaulting his eardrums. He threw off the headphones, shot back from the table and stared at the phonograph.

'Are you all right?'

He jumped, his hand clutched to his chest, breathing ragged. The voice was in the room with him. Eve was standing in the kitchen doorway.

The shadow disappeared.

Eve looked at him. 'Are you all right?'

He didn't reply.

She nodded towards the phonograph. 'Any joy?'

'No,' said Harry, 'far from it.'

The Key

Eve stood by the window in the hallway, looking out at the causeway; that long stretch of half-submerged road stretching back to civilisation. When she thought of the house and everything that had been going on in it, civilisation seemed even further away.

Harry caught her up. He had told her about his experiences with the phonograph, letting her listen for herself. After doing so she had walked out of the kitchen, deep in thought.

She turned to him now. 'Could that have been who I saw?' she said. 'Jennet? I saw her gravestone.'

Harry frowned. 'The way Alice spoke, it didn't

sound as if Jennet was real. The recording was very poor but it sounded like Alice was blaming her own guilty conscience. Imagining things.'

'But I saw someone. In the graveyard.'

'Yes, but you said yourself that she disappeared when you tried to follow her.' He tried to laugh, failed. 'I mean, really, if I didn't know better, I would say she was a . . .'

'Ghost?' asked Eve, eyes locked on to his. 'Is that what you were going to say?'

Harry shook his head in exasperation. The children were supposed to be working, but they were all staring through the open doorway at the two of them. After what had happened, neither of them could blame them for being scared and curious.

He hoped they couldn't hear what he and Eve were talking about. 'What about the key?' he asked. 'Have you . . . have you had any luck?'

'No,' said Eve. 'I've tried it everywhere, every lock I could find in the whole house. Even the ones I didn't think it would fit. Nothing. Whatever it opens isn't here.'

Harry shrugged. 'Then wherever it fitted wasn't here in the first place.'

'Perhaps,' said Eve, frowning, trying to recall

something. 'But I've seen those letters somewhere before, I'm sure of it.'

'Someone at school? Someone in your family, perhaps?'

She shook her head. 'No, it's since I've been here . . .'

She looked back at the causeway, stretching to the village of Crythin Gifford and beyond.

Crythin Gifford . . .

She glanced at the key clutched in her hand, at the initials 'HJ', then back to Harry. 'The village.'

He looked puzzled. 'Really? You're sure?'

'Yes. Definitely. I went there the night we arrived. I . . . Yes. Those initials. I saw them in the village.' She looked through the double doors at the children. They immediately pretended to be working once more. 'I'll tell Jean we're going now. She can take the class.'

A ghost of a smile appeared on Harry's lips, accompanied by a twinkle of humour in his eye. 'Would you like some moral support with Sergeant Battleaxe?'

'No, thank you,' said Eve, blushing slightly, 'I'll be fine.'

'Good,' he said, heading towards the front door.

'Then I'll get the Jeep started.'

Eve walked towards the children's dormitory to talk to Jean. Before she reached the door she turned.

And saw someone at the end of the corridor.

A figure, all in black.

Eve's heart skipped a beat. She froze to the spot. The figure didn't move.

'Jean?' Eve asked, her voice smaller than she had intended.

The figure remained motionless.

Eve felt her legs and arms begin to tremble. 'Get out . . .' The words came out in a hissed whisper.

She moved slowly along the corridor towards it.

'Get out . . .' She had found her voice now. She moved faster, anger overtaking fear until she stood right before the figure.

'I said, get out!'

She pulled her arm back, let go a punch at the figure.

To find that it was a coat hanging on a peg.

Eve stepped back, shaken.

'No . . . no . . .'

She turned round to find Jean standing in the corridor, staring at her, features impassive.

'A word, please?'

Jean walked back into the children's dormitory. Eve, dumbfounded, followed.

Jean shook her head vigorously as if trying to dislodge something that shouldn't be in there, a thought that she found alien to her belief system.

'No,' she said, unwilling and unable to countenance what Eve was telling her. 'No, no, no. Absolute poppycock.'

'It's not, Jean,' said Eve, trying to be patient and not let the exasperation show in her voice. She faced Jean across one of the beds. There was more than just physical space between them. 'Whoever she is, we — that's Harry and I — think she had something to do with Tom's death.'

'Oh, Harry and I. Of course.'

'Jean, please, just listen . . .'

'No,' said Jean, snapping at her, eyes fiery. 'No. You listen. Listen to yourself. You should hear what you sound like.'

Eve sighed. 'Look, Jean, I know it must sound mad . . .'

'Yes, it does. Sounds it and looks it.'

Jean spoke as if that were the end of the argument. Eve pressed on.

'Jean, please. She seems to be trying to talk to Edward, to communicate with him in some way.'

Jean drew in a sharp breath, used it to hold her posture in its usual military bearing before she spoke. 'Do you want to know what I think this is?' Her voice was no longer angry. There was still the usual authoritarianism, but it was tempered by a kind of compassion. 'I think you're looking for any way not to blame yourself.'

Eve felt tears prick behind her eyes and was determined not to let them fall. 'That's not true . . .'

'Miss Parkins . . .' Jean put her head to one side and spoke slowly, spelling things out for her. 'It is my belief that you are not suited to this. And I don't want you to blame yourself. If anything, it's my fault for bringing you here.'

'No . . .' Eve shook her head. 'No . . . I can't leave them here. I won't.'

'And yet,' said Jean, continuing in the same calm, rational voice, 'you now want to abandon your duty of care to them and go to the village with the captain.' She smiled. It wasn't pleasant. 'Do you see what I mean?'

'I . . . I . . . no. It's not like that. I have to go

to . . .' Eve swallowed hard. 'I'm going there now. That's all I came to say.'

Jean nodded, her features hard, cold. 'Very well. But should you choose not to return, I would find that perfectly acceptable.'

Eve had a retort planned but thought better of it. Instead she went to join Harry.

Survivors

Harry watched the road ahead. Eve watched Harry.

The RAF captain was tense, his hands gripping the wheel so hard his knuckles were rigid and white. The charming, smiling young man she had become used to had disappeared. In his place was a wild-eyed bundle of nerves. He drove the Jeep at great speed across the causeway.

'Harry . . .' She spoke gently, not wanting to disturb him but hoping that he would take notice of her and slow down. She was becoming frightened.

'I received a message on the radio,' he said, eyes never leaving the road ahead. 'I'm needed back at the airfield. I'm afraid I can only drop you off and pick you up in a couple of hours. Will that be all right?'

'Yes,' she said, 'that should be fine.'

Harry gave a curt nod. Eve noticed that the sweat on his forehead was beginning to run down his face.

'Harry, is everything all right?'

'Fine,' he said, his voice slightly too loud and too high. He still wouldn't look at her. 'The tide's coming in. We have to hurry.'

Eve looked out of the window. The sun was high, the sky clear and the snow had started to melt. The water was calm, hardly even lapping at the edges of the causeway.

'It's fine,' she said.

'No, it's not,' he snapped, and pushed his foot harder on the accelerator.

Eve gripped tightly to the edges of her seat. 'Harry, please . . .'

He drove even faster, his eyes mad, staring, focused not on the road but at something far beyond it.

'Please, slow down . . .'

Harry took deep breaths while he drove. He was trying to keep himself calm. He hit the steering wheel hard. Once, twice, three times. It didn't seem to work.

Eve turned to him. 'Harry . . .'

'Quiet!' He shouted the word out.

Eve flinched, shocked by the ferocity in his voice.

'Sorry, I . . .' The words seemed unconvincing, even to him. 'I need to concentrate . . .'

The Jeep went even faster. Eve held on to her seat, closed her eyes.

Eventually they reached the other side and Harry brought the Jeep to a halt. He slumped forward over the steering wheel, breathing hard as if he had just finished a marathon. He was shaking.

Eventually he regained control of himself, wiped the sweat from his forehead, swallowed hard.

'I suppose,' he began, his voice cracked, hesitant. 'I suppose I owe you an explanation.'

'No, it's . . .'

He gave a sad smile. 'Please. Don't be polite. I was awful back there.'

Eve said nothing, just waited.

'We got . . . shot down. Over the sea. My crew were trapped in the fuselage as it . . . as it went under . . .' Harry stared out of the windscreen, eyes focused on somewhere Eve couldn't see, didn't want to see. 'I swam down to rescue them. They were . . . were calling to me . . . "Help me . . . Help me, Captain" . . . and I could see them, I was . . . I was almost . . .' He shut his eyes tight, let go a breath he hadn't noticed he was holding. 'It was sinking too fast. I . . . I couldn't reach them.'

Despite the brightness of the day, he seemed to be in shadow.

Eve searched for the right words. 'I'm . . .'

'I was the only survivor.'

Neither of them spoke; they just sat there, staring ahead. Then Harry turned to Eve.

'So now I don't like the water.' His voice aimed for lightness. Missed.

Eve said nothing. Just placed her hand gently over his.

Edward's Conversation

Jean looked anxious. Her eyes were darting about nervously and she kept knitting and unknitting her fingers as the children filed into the dining room for their next lesson. They all noticed her out-of-character behaviour. That, combined with the absence of Miss Parkins and the death of Tom, had unsettled them greatly.

'Come on,' Jean said, attempting to chivvy them along, 'break-time is over.' She looked round the group, making yet another head count. 'Where's Edward?' Panic rose in her voice.

'He was on his bed, reading,' said Joyce.

Jean stared at her, fear expressing itself as anger

in her features, her voice. 'What did I say about rules? Hmm? What did I say?'

Joyce just stared back, unsure whether the question was rhetorical or not.

'Go and fetch him, please, Joyce.'

'Yes, Headmistress.' And Joyce ran off.

Joyce put her head round the double doors, ready to shout at Edward, mimic Mrs Hogg's authoritarian manner, but the room was empty. She checked every corner, even looking under the beds in case he was playing some kind of hide-and-seek. She avoided Tom's bed, though. The mattress had been stripped, the blankets removed. It stood bare and lonely at the end of the room. Joyce noticed that the black rot had spread so much on the wall behind it that it looked like a permanent shadow was standing over the bed. She shivered. It gave her the creeps.

In fact, the whole house gave her the creeps. But Mrs Hogg was right. The only way they were going to get through this was to follow the rules. Joyce had learned that at a very early age at home. Both her parents enjoyed having a good time, so much so that bills often went unpaid and groceries had to be negotiated for. Her father had gone to fight, leaving her mother to bring up Joyce. She spent most of her time in the pub, drinking away what little money they had.

Joyce decided she would never end up like that. Thank goodness for Mrs Hogg. Joyce loved and admired her, wanted to be like her when she grew up. She had taken to ensuring she was always dressed smartly for school, even if she had to wash her clothes herself, and always arrived there on time. In fact, she regarded Mrs Hogg as more of a mother to her than her actual mother was. She would never dream of telling Mrs Hogg that, though. That wasn't in her rules.

She heard a floorboard creak and looked round. Not in the room. She heard it again. Upstairs. That was where it was coming from. Edward must be up there.

She left the room and made her way up the creaking staircase, stopping at the top. She saw Edward at the end of the corridor, standing on the threshold of the nursery, the room Tom had locked him in yesterday. He had that horrible puppet thing in his hand. Joyce hated it. Every time she looked at it, its teeth seemed to be blacker and more rotten, its grin wider and more unpleasant.

Edward hadn't seen her. Joyce started to walk towards him. He had the puppet up to his ear, as if listening to it. Then he nodded and held the puppet out, as if he was talking through it to someone else in the room. A quick shake of his head, then the puppet was at his ear again. He paused, nodded again. Joyce could hear a faint hissing sound while he did this, like something sliding about in water. She could smell something too. Rotten, like old fish.

'Edward?' she said.

He jumped, put the puppet behind his back, stared at her, round-eyed.

Joyce tried to see round him into the room. 'Who were you talking to?'

Edward ignored her and, pushing past her, walked off along the corridor and down the stairs.

Joyce opened her mouth to say something, admonish him for his rudeness, but she decided against it. He had been through a great trauma, which had obviously upset him in some way. Instead she looked at the open doorway. Should she go in and investigate? See if there was someone in there, someone he had been talking to? Or had he just been playing, making up an imaginary friend?

Her foot was on the threshold, ready to step inside, when a strange feeling overwhelmed her. It was like she felt when she looked at the black rot behind Tom's bed: creepy and lonely. Scared. She pulled her foot back and ran quickly back down the corridor, to Mrs Hogg and safety.

No Goodbyes

The sun was almost gone by the time Harry pulled the Jeep up by the church on the edge of Crythin Gifford. Eve got out and looked round at the ruined village. The gathering dusk caused the shadows to lengthen, the village to darken, as if some giant, taloned hand was grasping it in its clutches.

Harry leaned out of the driver's side window. He was clearly torn between anguish at leaving Eve there on her own and worry at disobeying orders. 'I'm sorry I can't stay,' he said. 'Truly.'

'Don't worry,' said Eve. 'I'm sure I'll be fine.'

Harry nodded, wanting to believe her.

'I think it's admirable, you know,' she said. 'I mean that.'

Harry frowned. 'What's admirable?'

Eve's eyes drifted towards the sky. 'That you still go up there. After what happened.'

'You have to carry on, don't you?' he said, his voice trailing away.

Eve nodded. 'Yes. You're right.' She smiled. 'Good lu—'

'Don't,' he said sharply. 'Wishing luck is bad luck. And no goodbyes. Ever. They're forbidden, too.'

He offered her a pale smile and drove away.

She stood watching him go. No goodbyes, she thought. What must it be like to wave someone off, thinking it could be the final time you would see them, and knowing that they were thinking the same thing? Would you both pretend that nothing was happening? Would you both lie to each other? And if you did, what would that do to a person? How could you carry on? She shook her head. This war had a lot to answer for.

She turned and walked away from the retreating Jeep, through the village.

She knew where she was headed.

HJ

Eve stood before the burned-out exterior of the building and checked the sign:

Mr Horatio Jerome M.S. Esq.,

Solicitor.

Then she looked at the key she held in her hand. 'HJ' was inscribed on it in the same font that had been used on the sign.

The receding sun caused the shadows to lengthen, made the blackened front windows look like two ghostly, haunted eyes, the doorway a gaping maw.

Clutching the key tightly before her, like a crucifix to ward off vampires, she stepped inside.

The inside of the building had been so blackened by fire that it seemed to make what light remained of the dying day hasten away. For a fleeting second she thought of the black mould and rot covering the walls of Eel Marsh House. *This is what it'll look like eventually*, she thought.

She stood in the hallway. The offices were panelled half in wood and half in glass and ran the length of one side, with what remained of a staircase heading downwards at the opposite end. The wallpaper was charred black and mildewed green. To one side of Eve was a large hole in the floorboards, its edges black, where she could see right into the basement. She walked to the edge of the hole and looked down, but saw only further ruin, swirling dust.

Entering the nearest office, she checked it for anything that the key might fit but found nothing. She checked the next office along, came up with the same result. She then made her way down the staircase into the basement.

The first thing she noticed was a charred, built-up pile in the centre of the room, looking like the remains of a bonfire. Eve frowned. Had the fire been started deliberately?

The blackened pile still held vague shapes. Eve carefully peered into it, checking for anything that might have a keyhole among the debris — a locked box, perhaps — but she could see nothing.

Then something caught her eye. She picked it up. An old doll, soot-covered and singed. It looked like Judy, the companion to Edward's Mr Punch puppet. There was no joy in the doll's face. Its eyes were wide and fearful, its mouth a shocked O. With a shiver, Eve threw it back where she had found it.

As she did so, she noticed a small archway in the far corner, covered by a metal gate, fire-blackened and rusted, but still looking substantial and solid. Eve pulled at it. With a creaking of ancient, disused hinges, it opened. Eve walked through it and found herself in a narrow corridor. At the end of it was a stack of safety deposit boxes. Eve felt her heart skip, and the key in her hand suddenly felt hot.

She tried the key in the first box. It fitted but didn't turn. She tried it in the next one. The same thing happened.

The third one opened.

Dread mingling with excitement, she reached inside, removed what was there.

An envelope.

She read the name and inscription: *Nathaniel Drablow, on his eighteenth birthday.* She turned it over. It had a wax seal on the back and had never been opened.

The gate clanged shut. Startled, she turned to see a figure silhouetted against the dying light. She heard rather than saw a lock being turned, and ran to the gate.

'You can't go back,' said a rasping, cracked voice. 'I'm sorry.'

Eve recognised the old, blind man she had seen when she arrived in the village. He was much bigger, much stronger than she had first realised. She pulled at the gate, but it held fast.

'What are you doing?' she said, her voice tinged with hysteria and disbelief. 'You can't do this. You can't lock me in here and leave me . . .'

He turned and began walking down the corridor.

'Please,' she shouted, her voice echoing round the walls. 'Please . . . come back . . .'

He stopped, but didn't turn to face her. 'If you go back to the house,' he said, his voice heavy as if the reluctant deliverer of an unpleasant message, 'the killings will start again . . .'

'What d'you mean?' asked Eve.

'You heard my friends . . .' He nodded along with his words.

'Your friends?'

'Yes . . . they sang you their song . . .'

Eve remembered. The children's voices, the choir she had heard the first time she entered the village. Heard but not seen.

'Yes,' said Eve. 'I heard them.'

'Well, you should have listened.' He continued towards the stairs.

Eve knew she had to do something, say something, to get him to come back and let her out.

'It's her, isn't it?' she called. 'Jennet Humfrye. That's who you're talking about.'

The old man froze. But still he wouldn't turn to face her. 'Lost her boy Nathaniel in the marsh,' he said, his voice now quavering and faint. 'Then killed herself. But she came back for the other children. Oh, yes . . .'

Eve tried to keep him talking. Not just to get him to let her out, but also because she wanted to know. 'But how does she . . .'

He talked over the top of her, reciting a verse. Eve wasn't sure if he had made it up himself.

'Whenever she's seen, and whomever by, one thing's certain, a child shall die.' He shook his head. 'So true, so true . . . And that's why I can't allow you to go back to the house.'

Eve nodded, taking his words in. 'But,' she said, 'a child has died already.'

The old man slowly turned back to face Eve.

His sightless eyes staring at her.

James

James sat in the classroom unable to concentrate on his work. Tom's death had upset them all, but he seemed to feel it most keenly. Since they had left London Tom had become his friend, and, although he wasn't entirely sure he liked him, a friend was a friend and you were meant to be upset when something like this happened.

He wanted to run away, as far and as fast as possible. But he knew he couldn't. He could hardly leave the house without Mrs Hogg's say-so, so he sat there, fidgeting with nervous energy and apprehension.

He looked over at Edward, the boy who used to be his best friend. He didn't know what had happened. It wasn't just Edward losing his mother, it was everything. He knew he should keep trying to do nice things for Edward, but what was the point? Edward had changed, and he had to accept it.

He looked down at his work. He couldn't do any more writing, and he couldn't sit here any longer. He put his hand up.

'Miss,' he said, trying to attract Mrs Hogg's attention, 'I'm hungry.'

Jean put down her knitting and looked at him over the top of her reading glasses. 'Finish your work.' She returned to her needles.

James put his hand up again. 'Miss,' he said.

Jean looked up once more, irritated this time. 'Yes, James.'

'I've finished.'

She sighed. 'Then write it out again.'

'But Miss Parkins lets us—'

'Miss Parkins is not here!' Jean slammed the knitting down on the table with such force that the rest of the class jumped. Jean seemed to regret her loss of composure, took a few seconds and gathered herself. 'I have no concern as to what Miss Parkins lets you do. You will do as I say. Now be quiet and write it out again.'

The knitting was resumed.

James couldn't sit still. His right foot was bouncing up and down so hard he felt it might fall off. He had an idea and stuck his hand in the air once more.

'Miss,' he said.

Jean was getting angry now and was about to shout at him or hand him some punishment, but he continued talking.

'I need to go to the toilet, Miss.'

Jean sighed and shook her head. 'Go,' she said. 'Just go.'

Outside the room, James looked up and down the hallway. Instead of going to the toilet as she would expect him to do, he turned right and headed towards the kitchen, smiling to himself at how clever he had been.

Unaware of the dark-clothed figure watching him from the top of the stairs.

Hunt at Night . . .

'What . . . what's your name?'

Eve stared at the sightless eyes before her. She knew she had to get his attention, talk him round. Make him unlock the gate. She had dealt with enough children's tantrums to know how to calm someone down. She should be able to deal with this old man.

'My name?' he said, as if it were a question he hadn't been asked for years and had to think about. 'Jacob.'

'Jacob,' she said. She smiled, knowing he couldn't see it but hoping that the lift would show in her voice. 'Hello. I'm Eve. How long have you lived here, Jacob?'

He flicked his head around as if bothered by a troublesome fly. 'Always . . .'

'I thought everyone had left the village?'

He nodded. 'They did. I'm the last. The last . . .'

Eve leaned forward. 'What do you mean?'

'Dead.' He spat the word out like gristle. 'All the others are dead.' His laugh was high-pitched and unhinged. 'But she couldn't catch me.' He pointed to the milky dead orbs of his eyes. 'Born like this . . .' He wiped his fingers across his eyes and didn't blink.

'So how did you survive, Jacob?'

He pointed to his eyes once more. 'Because of these . . .'

'Right. And how do you still survive?'

'Hunt. At night.' He leaned closer. She could smell the rankness of him. 'When eyes don't mean nothing . . .'

Eve breathed deeply through her mouth. 'Jacob,' she said, trying to appear calm and reasonable. 'I need to go and take the children from the house. I need to keep them safe. I can't just leave them there.'

Jacob's face took on a thoughtful expression. He moved towards the gate. Emboldened by this, Eve continued.

'I saw her, Jacob. That means she's coming again, doesn't it?'

Jacob stopped, shook his head. 'No . . . no, no, no . . .'

'Jacob,' said Eve, urgency in her voice now, 'listen to me. I promise if you let me go and get the children, take them to safety, we'll leave and never come back.'

He let out a sound like a wounded animal. 'Too late,' he said, 'too late . . .'

'Please,' said Eve, panic rising within her, 'please, Jacob, let me go . . .'

Jacob lunged for the gate. His hands went straight through the bars and grabbed hold of Eve. Stunned and unable to fight back, she felt him pulling her towards him, crashing her against the metal.

'Too late . . . too late . . .'

James thought he was being really clever. He hadn't lied to Mrs Hogg, not really. Well, not about being hungry, that bit was true. And he probably did need to go to the toilet, just not yet. He had to get something to eat first.

He opened the door to the walk-in larder in the kitchen and stood before the shelves, deciding what to take. There wasn't a great deal of choice, but, he thought, beggars can't be choosers. He found a few oatcakes and stuffed them into his pocket. They were for later, when he couldn't sleep and woke up peckish, but they wouldn't do now. He looked for something more.

The dark-clothed woman with the bleached-bone face entered the kitchen, the walls cracking and blackening as she approached. She brought with her the sound of the eels slithering in the water beyond the island, and the faint smell of decay.

So engrossed was he in his task that James didn't notice the presence behind him. But he did see what he wanted. A jar of toffees on the top shelf.

James started to climb.

She Gets Inside Your Head . . .

Jacob pulled Eve's face right up against the bars. She was only inches away from him. She could smell his unwashed skin, his decayed teeth, his rancid clothing. She was so close she could see tiny insects moving about on his scalp.

'She gets inside your head,' Jacob was saying, spraying Eve with tiny flecks of spittle. 'Makes you do things . . . All the little girls and boys, with sparkly eyes and teeth like pearls . . .'

Eve was trying to look anywhere, everywhere, but at his face. Her eyes cast about, settled on his belt. There was a large key stuffed into it. Hope rose within her then, faint as it was. *Keep him talking,* she thought. *Keep him talking.*

'If that's the case,' she said, 'then tell me how we can stop her.'

Jacob began to jerk his head around as if a different beat, one Eve couldn't hear, had taken him over. 'Drowns . . . burns . . . poisons . . . cuts . . .'

Slowly, she reached her hand down towards the key.

'Jacob . . . Jacob . . . You have to help me . . . The children . . .'

'Nobody's seen her for years . . .' His voice was getting louder, wilder, his head swings more erratic. 'You broke that. *You.* Now she's getting stronger.' He pulled Eve even closer to him. 'I can feel it.'

Eve tried not to breathe in his foul breath. 'But, Jacob, please, there must be a way we can . . .'

She grabbed the key.

'Thief,' he shouted. 'Thief . . . You . . . you steal from me . . .'

He pushed her back from the gate, sending her sprawling on to the rough floor. Then he stepped back from the gate and, with a scream, ran at it. It buckled slightly but didn't budge. He moved further down the corridor, then came at it once more, screaming louder this time. The gate, old and rusted, started to come loose. He tried a third time. The ancient lock gave and the gate swung open, clattering against the wall.

Eve lay still, staring upwards. Jacob stood in the archway, blocking her escape.

The gate was open, but she was still trapped.

James stood on the middle shelf and reached his hand up to the next one. *Why would someone put a jar of toffees all the way up here? To stop me from getting them,* he answered himself. He smiled. *Didn't work, did it?*

As his hand groped higher, his smile withered and died. His features became impassive, blank, his eyes unblinking. His hand stopped moving and he turned, sensing a presence behind him. He nodded once as if in response to an unheard command and turned back to the larder.

He climbed to the next shelf and reached up to the very top one. There was very little there apart from dust, mouse droppings, and a jar with a skull and crossbones on it. Rat poison.

Behind him, the woman's eyes glittered with dark malevolence.

Never Go Back . . .

Jacob advanced into the room, head on one side, listening.

'You don't go back,' he said, 'you can never go back, never . . .'

Eve looked frantically round, assessing her options. She saw her only chance and took it, scrambling quickly round Jacob on all fours while he regained his balance and breath after breaking the gate. He sensed immediately what was happening, and bent down to grab her. But she was too quick for him. She managed to wriggle past him, and, pulling herself to her feet, she attempted to run down the corridor and away from him.

Jacob anticipated her move and stuck out a foot. Eve tripped and fell face down on to the floor, winded.

Jacob moved quickly. Eve knew she had to get up. Acknowledging the pain in her chest was a luxury that she couldn't afford. She crawled as fast as she could down the corridor to the first room. She saw the charred remains of the bonfire and looked round, trying to find something she could use against him. Her eyes alighted on the Judy puppet.

Picking it up as quietly as possible, and making no sound as she managed to get upright, she threw it across the room in the direction she had come from.

Jacob spun quickly round.

Eve, heart pounding, ran for the spiral staircase.

She made it back up to the ground floor, Jacob screaming abuse below her. She hoped the noise he was making would cover her movement as she edged slowly round the broken floorboards, but Jacob heard her, his hands coming up over the edge, trying to grab her, pull her back down with him, trying to grab her, pull her back down with him.

'You . . . can't . . . go . . . back . . .'

Eve reached the door, made it out of the

building and ran down the street. She could hear
Jacob screaming behind her, but she didn't stop,
didn't look back. She kept running, running.

Until she collided with another person.

Eve screamed.

'Hello, old girl. You in a spot of bother?'

Harry.

Eve had never been more relieved to see anyone
in her life.

James reached out as far as he could, his fingers
finding the rat poison. He pulled the jar closer to
himself and began to open it.

Suddenly, he was pulled back from the shelf.

He blinked, as if awaking from a deep sleep, and
turned. There stood Mrs Hogg.

'What are you doing?' she said.

James looked round the kitchen. He had no idea
where he was or how he had got there. He vaguely
remembered someone else being with him. Was
that right? If so, they weren't there now.

'Go and join the rest of the children, please, and
leave the toffees alone.'

James, still dazed, nodded dumbly and left the
kitchen.

Jean, about to leave, noticed the patch of black mould on the wall. She examined it with disgust.

'This place is falling apart,' she said, and followed James from the room.

Nathaniel

The Jeep bumped and rolled as Harry floored the accelerator, trying to get back to Eel Marsh House as fast as possible. Eve had told him what had happened in the old solicitor's house. He had been so shaken by what she said that it had temporarily taken away his fear of driving over the causeway through the rising tide.

Eve held the letter in her hand, Harry's cigarette lighter illuminating it. 'Nathaniel died before he turned eighteen,' she said.

'So he never read the letter?' asked Harry, facing front, concentrating on the pitch-black road ahead.

'No, he didn't.' She opened it, held the lighter

close enough to see the wording and read it out. '"Dear Nathaniel, I do not have much time. They are sending me to an asylum, so when you read this I shall be long gone."' She turned to Harry. '"They".' She kept reading. '"I am writing so you will know the truth."' She read on, silently. 'Oh, dear God . . .'

'What does it say?'

She cleared her throat, read it aloud. '"You were brought up to think that Alice Drablow was your mother, but she is not. Your father is indeed Charles Drablow. But *I* am your real mother. This is the truth. They took you from me and I was powerless to stop them. Please believe what I say and come to rescue me as soon as you can. They would not allow me close contact with you, but I have always watched over you and loved you from a distance. If I have gone mad it is mad from grief over what they have done to me and how they have kept me apart from you. For I was, am, and always shall be, your mother. Jennet Humfrye."'

Eve put down the letter and clicked the lighter shut. They both sat in silence, taking in what she had just read. Subconsciously Eve's fingers began to caress her cherub necklace.

'He never knew she was his mother. Never knew . . .'

Her eyes were wet and glistening.

Harry kept his attention on the road.

'We'll get them out of there. We've got to.'

He pushed his foot down hard on the accelerator. The Jeep splashed through the causeway towards the island.

Night Falls

Joyce was seriously worried. She had come down-stairs after seeing Edward standing in the doorway to the upstairs room. She knew something was wrong with him, desperately wanted to tell Mrs Hogg about it. But every time she had tried to do so, Mrs Hogg had brushed her off in an irritated fashion, and now it was bedtime.

Mrs Hogg watched over the children as they climbed into their beds. Joyce tried hard not to look at the empty bed where Tom had been. She was sure the mould had increased around it.

'Chop-chop, children,' said Mrs Hogg, 'come along into bed.'

Just the sort of thing she herself would say one day when she was a teacher, thought Joyce.

They heard the sound of a Jeep approaching and sprang to attention, looking at one another, suddenly excited.

'Settle down,' said Jean, heading towards the door. 'I want everyone in their beds by the time I get back.' She hurried out of the room.

Joyce was concerned. Mrs Hogg usually seemed to be in charge all the time. No matter what was going on, she dealt with it in a calm and unruffled manner. Tonight she seemed distracted and nervous, almost running outside when she heard the sound of the Jeep. That wasn't like her.

Most of the children, Joyce noted with disdain, had ignored Mrs Hogg and, instead of getting into bed, made their way to the window to see what was going on. Joyce had to admit that she wanted to do the same thing, but Mrs Hogg had given them an instruction and they had to put aside what they wanted to do because Mrs Hogg knew what was best for them. So Joyce crossed over to the window with the others, ready to tell them off, while snatching a quick look at what was happening for herself.

As she walked past Edward's bed she noticed,

next to that revolting Mr Punch doll, that his drawing was there, the one of a mother and son. The one that Tom had taken from him.

She picked it up and walked over to Edward, who was looking out of the window with the rest of the children.

'How did you get this?'

She held it out towards him. Edward turned, surprised. He glanced down at the drawing then back up at her.

'Tom had it in his pocket the night that he died. How did you get it back?'

Edward didn't answer. The children had stopped watching the Jeep pull up, and Miss Parkins and the RAF captain get out, and decided this was more interesting.

Joyce nodded, her mind made up. 'I'm going to tell Miss.'

Edward snatched the drawing from her and hurried back to his bed.

Joyce left the room. Mrs Hogg would have to listen to her now.

Eve could hear a rushing, roaring sound, but she wasn't sure if it was the waves starting to encroach on the causeway and the muddy shingle of the beach, or the blood hurrying round her body as her heart pounded.

She and Harry were standing beside the Jeep. They hadn't managed to get inside the house as Jean had marched out to meet them, her expression as impassive and unmoving as an ancient marble death mask. Eve had been trying to tell her what had happened in the village, impart what they had discovered, but Jean wasn't making it easy.

'Whenever she is seen,' Eve said, starting again, 'a child dies. That's her curse. She lost her own child, so she took revenge on the village by killing all their children. And now we've arrived here, it's started again . . .'

Jean shook her head, face still expressionless but her eyes blazing. 'Oh, don't be so . . .'

At that moment, Joyce ran outside the house.

'Mrs Hogg, Mrs H—'

'Get back inside!' Jean screamed at the girl.

Joyce, momentarily stunned, her bottom lip quivering, went back inside.

Eve took the opportunity to press her point home. 'We have to leave now. Right away. Before the tide comes in.'

'Don't be ridiculous,' said Jean. 'We can't cross a flooding causeway in the dark.'

'Harry can drive us, then,' said Eve. He gave a small nod.

Jean turned to him, her mask slipping, her voice hissing. 'This is none of his business,' she said.

'Look, Jean,' said Eve, trying to recapture the headmistress's attention. 'Edward saw her in the nursery yesterday and Tom died. And now I've seen her. Today. So that means—'

'You,' said Jean, pointing a wavering finger in Eve's face, 'you need to think straight . . .'

Harry turned away from both of them and looked up into the night sky.

Eve dropped her voice, trying to be reasonable. 'Please, Jean, I'm telling you that—'

'No!' Jean shook her head once more, clenching and unclenching her fists. She began to walk round in tight circles, her shoes crunching on the gravel. 'I have survived this war by being rational. And more than ever, that is what these children need. A rational voice. That is what we *all* need.' She stopped right in front of Eve, face to face. Her voice was shaking with emotion. 'Is that . . . is that clear?'

Eve stepped away from her, stunned by her reaction. She had never seen Jean behave like this in all the time she had known her, never known her to be so close to losing control. Before she could speak, Harry turned back to them.

'We can't leave,' he said.

Jean gave a smile that was more of relief than triumph. 'Thank you, Captain,' she said.

Eve frowned, placed a hand on his arm. 'Harry . . .'

He pointed to the sky. 'Listen,' he said.

They did so and heard the familiar sound of a distant drone accompanied by a series of dead, dull thuds.

Eve turned back to him. 'But that sounds like . . .'

'A raid,' he said, 'yes.'

'What, all the way out here?' asked Eve.

Harry looked quickly round. 'We need to get to a shelter.'

'We don't have one,' said Jean.

Harry kept scanning the area. 'Anywhere underground, anywhere . . .'

'Well, there's the cellar,' said Jean.

'No,' said Eve. 'We can't stay here. And we certainly can't go down there.'

Harry placed his hands on her arms, looked right into her eyes. 'It'll have to do,' he said. 'Now come on, we don't have time to argue.'

The three of them hurried inside.

The sound of the approaching planes became louder.

The Raid

When they heard Jean hurry into the dormitory the children ran for their beds, except Joyce, who was already in hers. After Mrs Hogg had shouted at her she had come back into the room and got straight under the covers, not wanting the rest of the room to see how upset she was. That was it, as far as Joyce was concerned. She wouldn't speak to Mrs Hogg until she apologised to her.

The fact that Mrs Hogg wasn't cross with them for not being in their beds demonstrated that something serious was happening. Once she explained that there was a squadron of German bombers overhead, the children, grabbing their gas masks, knew exactly what to do.

'Down to the cellar,' said Jean, as they milled about, 'quickly.'

Eve entered the room with Harry. 'But why would they attack us? There's nothing here for miles around. Is it the airfield?'

'I doubt it,' said Harry, watching the children hurry from the room. 'Any bombs they haven't used on the cities they just drop on the way back. Pot luck, I'm afraid.'

Edward, in his haste to leave, had left Mr Punch behind.

'No time for that,' said Jean, grabbing his hand. 'Come on.'

The puppet was left on the bed, its broken-toothed grin leering at them, its once pristine braided tunic and hat now becoming as black and mouldy as the walls. Eve was glad the toy was staying where it was. Something about it unsettled her.

However, she didn't have time to dwell on that as the children had to be taken down to the cellar.

One by one they went, through the kitchen and

carefully down the slippery steps. Jean led them from the front, torch in hand. As Eve and Harry brought up the rear, herding the children before them, they heard Joyce shriek from below.

'Miss! Miss! It's all wet! And it stinks!'

Eve arrived at the bottom of the steps. Joyce was right. The water level in the cellar was even higher than earlier. It covered everyone's ankles, made its way up their legs.

'It will have to do,' said Jean, addressing the group. 'Everybody find something to sit or stand on. That should help. I'm afraid I can't do anything about the smell. The house is old; decay is every-where. You'll just have to get used to it.'

The children, theatrically holding their noses and making gagging noises, clearly didn't agree.

Ruby put her fingers on the nearest wall and felt the dripping, wet mould. 'It's horrible here, Miss. Even the walls are crying.'

Eve gave Harry a quizzical look. 'It's worse than before,' she said. 'It's no good, we have to get out of here.'

'We'll be fine if we stick together,' he said. 'Look out for each other.'

Eve nodded reluctantly.

'Come on, please,' said Jean, appearing at their side. 'Help the children.'

As Eve had expected, Jean was trying to cope with the stress of the situation by falling back on practicalities and routine. Her features were as impassive as they had been outside when Eve and Harry had told her about Jennet Humfrye. She organised everyone, making sure there were enough places to sit or at least stand in relative comfort.

'I suppose the encouraging thing is,' Jean said to no one in particular, possibly herself, 'that we don't have to be down here all night. Once the planes have passed, the danger should be over.'

No one answered. From above ground, they could hear the distant sound of falling bombs.

Candles had been lit and placed on any available surface. Everyone was shivering from the cold and the damp. The smell hadn't lessened, but they had all became accustomed to it. They couldn't sit anywhere central, so they had been forced to spread themselves out among the rows and racks, taking down the sturdiest of the boxes for seating, or perching on the edges of shelves.

'My mum,' said Ruby, 'says that when you can hear the bombs you've got nothing to worry about. It's when it goes quiet that they're going to drop on you.'

They all sat in silence, listening.

Tears in the Dark

Harry sat on an upturned crate and, trying to ignore the sound of the bombs falling outside, glanced over at Eve. After she had finished helping Jean organise the children she had sat on her own, taking out the letter from Jennet Humfrye and rereading it over and over, her features intent. *Like she's studying it*, he thought, *scrutinising it for some kind of hidden meaning or secret message.*

Harry didn't notice the boy sitting next to him.

'You a pilot?'

Harry jumped. He hadn't realised how nervous he felt. He turned to the boy. He was a pudgy child with curly hair, and his eyes were lit by both terror and excitement. Harry had seen plenty of people respond to war that way. Harry struggled to think. Alby? Something like that. Alfie. That was the boy's name.

'Miss Parkins says you're a pilot,' Alfie continued.

Harry nodded, as a bomb fell outside. They were coming nearer. 'That's right,' he said.

Alfie smiled. 'I'm going to be a pilot.'

The cellar shook as another bomb landed nearby. Harry winced. 'I'd wait until the war is over if I were you.'

The boy was gearing up to unleash all his questions, but Harry didn't want to answer them. He excused himself and stood up, making his way over to Eve, who was sitting with her back to the rest of the group, still poring over the letter. He sat down next to her, noticing, for the first time, the tears in her eyes.

'Hey,' he said, 'come on . . .' He put his arm round her.

'Nobody,' she said once she had her sobbing under control, 'nobody deserves to suffer like she did.'

She spoke in a whisper so that the others wouldn't hear her. Harry responded likewise.

'It's more than that, though, isn't it?' He studied her face. 'More than just Jennet Humfrye and her son.'

Eve didn't reply. Her hand went to the cherub necklace once more.

'Tell me why this has got to you,' he said.

She sighed, looking at him but not speaking. He took his arm away from her shoulder, held her hand. It felt cold, small.

'Please.'

Eve sighed again, her eyes darting round the cellar, checking no one was listening. As she started to talk, Harry stopped noticing the falling bombs.

'I . . . I had a child.' Her voice sounded as small as her hand felt, but it was anything but cold. 'A son. I wasn't married. We were . . . I was too young. So I . . . I gave him up.'

Her voice wavered.

Harry didn't know what to say. He stared at the light glinting off the necklace, at the smile of the shining, happy infant. Always there, always reminding her.

Eve held the letter out towards him. 'Jennet fought for her son.'

Harry was out of his depth. If he couldn't mend

something with his bare hands he didn't know what to do with it. But he wanted to help, wanted to say or do something that would give Eve some kind of peace.

'I'm sure you did the right thing,' he said, then castigated himself at the feebleness of his words.

Eve shook her head and continued. 'It was selfish, what I did. I thought . . . I thought I couldn't cope . . .' Her eyes glittered as she stared off into the past. 'A nurse came and took him away from me. Straight away. I never saw him. Never even held him. They wouldn't let me . . .' Her voice trailed away.

Harry waited.

'I tried to look for him, but they wouldn't tell me where he was. Wouldn't even tell me his name.' She sighed. 'So after a few years I . . . gave up. I gave up my own son. I let him go . . .'

Harry said nothing, just squeezed her hand.

'You can't let the past pull you under,' he said eventually. 'It's easy to let that happen, to allow yourself to become a prisoner of it, but you have to keep moving forward, keep going.' He sighed. 'I suppose what I'm trying to say is that . . . life is short and there's too much to do now. People around you need you, and you have to . . . you have to be . . .'

Eve looked deep into his eyes and she wondered whether he had been talking about himself as much as about her. Whatever it was, his words made her recognise something in him that was also in her. She threw her arms round him, pulled him close. He responded.

And then one of the children screamed.

Mother and Child

'What have I told you? What?'

Eve turned quickly, Harry's arms falling from her, and made her way across the cellar, the sloshing water round her ankles impeding her progress, drying her tears with the backs of her hands as she went. She found Fraser looking shamefaced, Jean before him.

'What did I tell you?' Jean continued. She pointed at a circular contraption on a shelf. 'Leave things alone.'

'Sorry, Miss,' he said, 'I just wanted to look through it . . .'

Fraser was holding an old zoetrope. Spin it

round fast enough and the drawn figures inside it start to move. He had looked through it and seen an angry face staring back at him from the other side. Jean's.

'Please replace it on the shelf, Miss Parkins.'

Eve took it from Fraser and returned it to the shelf. As she did so, she noticed a pile of old photographs next to it and picked them up. She undid the perished ribbon tying them together and, looking for something to take her mind off her earlier admission to Harry, began to look through them.

They depicted men and women dressed in what she assumed must have been their finest clothes, standing in formal, rigid poses, their features so unsmiling as to be almost angry. Under other circumstances she might have found them amusing. Eel Marsh House looked resplendent in all of them, solid and imposing, not the crumbling ruin it now was.

Then, in among them, folded up, she found another photograph. She opened it and felt a shiver of apprehension. It showed a mother and son standing in front of Eel Marsh House. The mother had her hand on the boy's shoulder, and the boy's hands were clasped together holding something.

The mother's eyes had been scratched out.

But that wasn't the only thing she found disturbing about the photograph. There was something familiar. Studying it further, she realised what it was. She had seen the picture before.

'Harry . . .'

He came over to her. 'What is it?'

She showed him the photograph. 'Look familiar? I've seen this before . . .'

'Where?' he whispered.

Eve nodded her head slightly in Edward's direction. He was sitting among the other children, but his stillness was holding him apart. His head was down, his attention focused on the picture in his lap.

'There,' she said, her voice as low as Harry's. 'Edward. The drawing he did, the one he won't let go of. I thought it was of him and his mother, but it's not.'

'Edward and . . .' He looked at her, shook his head. 'Not . . . Jennet?'

They both looked over at Edward. The boy slowly raised his head. His eyes, dark and hooded, found hers. Eve felt a chill once more. Then a look of fear crossed over Edward's face and he screwed his eyes tightly closed as if preparing for a painful blow.

'Edward . . .'

A sharp, cold breeze rushed through the cellar, blowing out all the candles. In the sudden darkness, the children screamed.

'It's all right, children,' said Jean, 'no need to panic. It's just a draught, that's all.'

Eve felt Harry next to her. He was moving, fumbling for his lighter.

'Remember where the matches are,' came Jean's voice. 'Remember . . . remember which shelf you put them on.'

Eve heard the sounds of splashing water as the children moved around, accompanied by whimpering as they struggled to hold down their mounting hysteria. She heard hands scrabbling as they searched for the matches.

She thought of Jacob, the blind hermit from the village. *At least they're safe,* she thought. *For now. At least she can't get them if they can't see her.*

'Miss,' shouted Ruby. 'I found some matches.'

Eve's heart skipped a beat.

Ruby's face was illuminated for a second, her shadow thrown against the back wall, as the match was struck, then quickly went out.

'I'll try again . . .'

Another ignition. This time, Eve saw Flora and Fraser standing next to her, their faces equally fearful, their three shadows cast against the wall. The match went out.

She tried again.

Edward, thought Eve, and hurried towards him, Harry at her side.

'Done it,' shouted Flora, lighting a candle from the match.

'Are we all here?' asked Jean. 'Good.'

They were all there. No one noticed the extra shadow, peeling away from the furthest corner of the cellar, moving towards them.

The light went out again.

'Ruby . . .' Jean's voice was fraught with tension. 'Come on . . .'

Ruby managed to get her candle relit. Once established, Jean took it from her and moved round the room, relighting the others. The tension in the room dropped. Some of the children laughed nervously.

'Stay close to us,' Eve said to Edward, smiling and putting her arm round him.

But Edward just shrugged her off.

Eve tried again. 'Please . . .' Edward did the

same thing. He didn't want her to touch him. Eve shook her head in exasperation and stepped back from him.

All of the children were now returned to the light.

Except one.

Joyce, unseen by the others, stood apart from the group. She had been hurt by Mrs Hogg's behaviour towards her, and even the sudden darkness hadn't managed to dispel that. Now she turned her head, looked into a corner where the shadows had gathered. She kept staring at that corner, unmoving. She did not scream or cry out. Something undulating and slimy writhed round her ankles. Her head was cocked on one side, as if she was listening. After a moment, hearing something no one else in the room could, she inclined her head in agreement. Slowly. Just once. Then she turned and, making as little noise as possible, as if whatever had been slithering round her ankles was now guiding her steps and cushioning her feet, walked towards the stairwell. She reached the foot of it, looked up.

Silhouetted against the doorway stood Jennet Humfrye.

She turned, walked away into the house.

Joyce, her features expressionless, her gait slow and measured, followed.

A Good Girl

The noise of the planes overhead was deafening, the house shaking from the close proximity of the dropping bombs. But Joyce didn't notice, didn't even flinch. She walked into the children's dormitory and over to her bed.

Jennet Humfrye stood in the corner behind Tom's stripped bed, the tendrils of black mould on the walls behind her rippling and grasping. Her posture erect, a black veil obscuring her bone-white features, the creases like long black tears streaking her face. Her eyes black coals, lit by a malevolent, dancing fire.

On the bed opposite Joyce was the Mr Punch

doll. Propped up against the pillow, it leered at her with its broken-toothed grin and scabbed, pustule-covered features.

Joyce paid no attention to either of them. She stopped by her bed and took her gas mask out of its case. Slowly, she unscrewed the filter and folded her wash cloth, pushing it inside, blocking the air passages.

She studied it, nodded. Pleased with her own handiwork.

Then pulled the mask over her head.

'Where's Joyce?'

Eve's voice echoed round the cellar.

Harry looked anxious. Eve saw something start to bend and snap behind Jean's eyes.

'Come on, everyone, search the cellar.'

The walls shook, dislodged dust and rot which floated down from the ceiling, but no one paid it any mind. They were intent on finding Joyce. They looked all through the cellar, down the gaps between shelves, into crevices, round corners. The girl was nowhere.

'She must have gone upstairs,' said Jean, looking up at the ceiling, anger building in her voice.

The walls shook as a bomb landed close by.

'We can't let her do that,' said Ruby, 'we have to find her . . .'

Eve tried to work out where Joyce had been. Over by the wall, near the staircase, that was it. She crossed over to the exact spot. The wall behind where Joyce had been standing was cracked, blackened. Eve's heart skipped a beat. She looked round at Harry.

'Jennet's taken her . . .'

Ruby frowned. 'Who's Jennet?'

Eve started to run up the stairs, Harry behind her.

Down below, the children began to panic.

'Everybody, stay where they are,' said Jean in her most authoritative voice. 'Everything is under control . . .'

But even she didn't believe her own words.

Joyce was trying to breathe but there wasn't enough air to fill her lungs.

She stood completely still, arms at her sides, breath rasping behind the gas mask's rubber, sucking it tighter to her face with each breath she attempted to pull in. She took another breath, tried again. But it was no good. There just wasn't enough air.

Joyce began to feel light-headed. As the bombs fell and exploded outside, she could see stars in front of her eyes. Her legs began to feel wobbly.

The eyeholes in the mask were becoming misty with her breathing. It was like her own personal fog. But through them she could just about glimpse the darkly dressed woman standing before her, the leering Mr Punch on the bed. She felt them both egging her on, encouraging her, and she wanted to please them both, especially the woman. She had strict rules, Joyce could sense it. And Joyce knew it was very important to stick to these rules. To do what the woman told her. To be a good girl.

She tried, and failed, to breathe once more.

The noise was deafening. The walls were shaking, the bombs falling. Eve shouted for Joyce, but she knew the girl wouldn't be able to hear her. She could barely hear herself.

She ran from the kitchen, Harry in tow, to the next room, then the next. They looked round desperately, shouting Joyce's name, dreading what they believed was happening, hoping they weren't going to be too late.

Joyce's legs gave way and she fell to the floor. The room was becoming dark, encroaching all around her. But this blackness wasn't like night, she knew that. This blackness would last for ever. But she had to do what the woman said. Had to follow her rules and please her.

The blackness overtook her, and Joyce felt a kind of relief. She had done what was asked of her. She had carried out her task perfectly. She heard a voice, as cracked and dark as the decaying house around her.

'That's the way to do it . . .'

'No. Oh, no. Oh, no, no, no, no, please, no . . .'
Eve and Harry ran into the children's dormitory. Joyce was lying on the floor, unmoving. Harry knelt down, ripped the gas mask off her and flung it across the room. Eve knelt beside him.

He tried to revive her, but from the colour of her face, from its twisted, contorted features, he knew that it was too late. Her eyes had rolled back into her head, leaving milky, dead-fish orbs staring at them.

Eve began to sob.

'It's all right,' said Jean from behind them, breathless from running. 'The planes are going. We're safe now. We're safe . . .'

She saw the lifeless body lying between them, and her voice died away.

Evacuees

'It was an accident, that's all, a terrible, terrible accident . . .'

Jean had always felt her opinions and beliefs were solid. She had made them so. She sometimes imagined her mind to be the tidiest place possible. Everything she felt and believed was in its place, perfectly ordered and nailed down tight. Anything unpleasant that she didn't want to – or couldn't – countenance was locked away, like unwanted bric-a-brac in a cupboard, things she couldn't get rid of but didn't want to see.

Now, after everything that had happened, every-thing she had witnessed, she felt those beliefs were shifting. They were no longer nailed down, safe and secure. They floated around, getting in the way, catching on things. The cupboard door was open, and those deep, dark thoughts were all spilling out. If she wasn't careful they would overwhelm her. Completely.

'A terrible, terrible accident . . .'

Jean spoke the words like a mantra, nodding each time she said them, as if by saying them enough times they would become the truth.

Outside, the sun, just coming up over the horizon, was promising a beautiful, crisp winter day. Glorious shafts of sunlight stabbed through the tall windows and illuminated the dining room in a bright and celestial manner. But the brightness didn't reach the figures sitting huddled round the table in as small a group as possible.

For want of anywhere else to put it, Joyce's body had been laid on her bed by Harry, a blanket covering it. The dormitory door had then been firmly closed, with strict instructions for no one to enter. The instructions were unnecessary. No one had wanted to.

Harry and Eve had taken charge of the remaining children, marshalling them into the dining room, insisting they keep together. The youngsters sat there in an almost catatonic state, apart from Ruby, who hadn't stopped sobbing. Harry and Eve sat with them, trying to think what to do next.

Jean's back was turned to the rest of the room. Not wanting anyone to see the tears she was desperately fighting back, determined not to give in to her emotions. For the first time in her life, her whole belief system had been challenged and she didn't know how to cope.

'It was an accident, that's all. Just a terrible, *terrible* accident . . .'

Harry placed his hand on her shoulder. 'Jean.'

She turned and looked at him, her lower lip trembling, eyes wild and unfocused.

'It wasn't,' he said, in as soft a voice as possible.

Silence fell. Even Ruby stopped crying.

Eve stood up. Helplessness, fear and anger were roiling within her, fighting for prominence. She had to do something, make some kind of move. She walked over to the nearest wall and slowly traced her fingers along a newly appeared crack, then pulled her fingers back and examined them as if she had been somehow contaminated.

That's it, she thought. *That's it.*

'What's the point?' she said, quietly.

She looked round the room, took in all the blackness, the cracks, that no amount of sunlight could ever reach.

'You're not going to bring him back!' she shouted. 'No matter how many you kill, he's not coming back!' She screamed the last three words.

The children just stared at her, fear in their eyes. They had never seen her like this before. First their headmistress, now Miss Parkins . . .

'Just . . . leave us alone . . .'

Harry got up and came to her, placing his arm round her shoulders. She felt her body slacken as tension ebbed away. He led her back to the table.

'We'll leave as soon as the tide clears,' he said. 'I can drive you to the village, then we'll work out how to get you all home.'

Eve stopped moving, shoulders tense once more. 'I'm not going back to the village,' she said.

Harry frowned.

'Take us to the airfield.'

Harry looked momentarily shocked at the suggestion. He appeared to be doing some calculations, she thought, like he was deciding on something.

Then he smiled. 'Fine,' he said.

*

The evacuation was in full swing. The children were being hurried out of the house as quickly as possible. They had packed only as much as they could carry in the Jeep. Edward, Eve noticed, was clutching Mr Punch firmly in his hand. It looked like it was deteriorating before her eyes. She didn't know how the boy could bear to touch it. She placed a hand on his arm, stopping him.

'We should leave that,' she said, as reasonably but firmly as she could. She managed the ghost of a smile. 'It belongs here.'

Edward didn't even acknowledge he had heard. He wouldn't let go of the toy.

'Give it to me, please, Edward.' Steel had entered her voice.

He shook his head.

'Edward . . .'

She made a grab for the doll, but he moved it away. She wasn't going to be beaten. With one hand she gripped Edward's arm tightly, with the other she pulled the doll from his grasp. As she did so, she felt a sharp pain in her hand. She gasped, dropping the doll and examining her fingers. She was bleeding between her thumb and forefinger.

Damn, she thought, *it's so old and cracked it's given me splinters.*

She picked the doll up and looked at it. The same leering grin was still in place, but this time there was blood between its teeth. If she didn't know better, she would have said that the doll had bitten her.

She threw it back into the house and turned to Edward. But he had silently joined the others in the Jeep.

Once they were all squeezed in, Harry got behind the steering wheel and drove away. Eve was sitting in the back with the children. While the rest of them were facing forward, she noticed Edward's head was turned, staring at the retreating house.

'Edward,' she said.

He looked at her, his eyes dark, unreadable.

'Don't look back,' she said.

She kept her eyes locked on his. Eventually he turned to face the front once more.

Rage. That was what was burning in the woman as she stood at the nursery window and watched them depart.

She stretched her fingers out, tried to touch them, reach them, bring them back. No good. They were too far away. Her fingers met the glass of the windowpane, her hand turned to a claw. The rage bubbled and burned within her, a life force feeding her, sustaining her continued existence.

She raked her fingers down the glass, her nails screeching and howling. The glass cracked into crazed razor patterns as she did so.

The Jeep disappeared over the causeway.

She let out a scream of wrath and pain as she watched them go, her fingers pressing harder on the fractured glass, the screeching increasing.

The window shattered into thousands of tiny shards; suddenly, explosively.

She would not let them get away.

The Phantom Airfield

'Planes!' shouted Alfie.

'Alfie, come back . . .' Jean's voice was lost on the wind, but she gave chase, wanting to keep them all together.

The boy, his earlier anxiety forgotten, had been excited as soon as he had glimpsed the planes through the fence as the Jeep approached the airfield. Once he had realised where they were headed, he had talked of nothing else all the way there.

Alfie ran as fast as he could towards the stationary planes dotted around the perimeter of the airfield, Jean and Eve close behind him. But he stopped dead as soon as he reached the first plane. Eve, panicking and fearing the worst, ran even faster to reach him.

As she came to a stop next to him he turned to her, disappointment and confusion on his face.

'They're not real. This isn't real . . .'

Eve looked round, seeing the airfield properly for the first time. Only then did she notice that it wasn't as she had imagined or expected an airfield to be. There were no hangars, just large sections of canvas stretched out upon the ground to give the impression of buildings from the air. The planes, while convincing from a distance, seen up close looked nothing of the sort. They were hollow, made from wood and canvas, their markings and engine parts merely painted on. All around the perimeter fence, scattered around the site, were large mesh baskets full of kindling.

A figure came out of a bunker buried in the side of the hill and strode towards them. Heavyset, in his forties, he was buttoning up his uniform tunic and loosening a linen napkin from around his neck. He stopped when he saw the women and children, frowned at Harry.

'What's going on, Corporal?' he said.

Eve looked at Harry, who reddened and cleared his throat.

'These people need to stay here for a few hours, Sergeant Cotterell. Evacuees. Their . . . house was destroyed in the bombing last night. I'm arranging transportation for them.'

Cotterell looked between Harry and the children, clearly unhappy with the situation. 'You should have cleared it with me, Corporal.'

Harry looked like he wanted to earth to open and swallow him up. 'Yes, Sergeant. I'm sorry.'

Cotterell found a last morsel of food stuck between his teeth, sucked it out, ate it. He nodded. 'Don't let them get in the way of your duties.'

'Sir.'

Cotterell drew in breath, expelled it slowly. 'The sitrep's all clear for tonight,' he said. 'So it's just you on watch. S-Team are on standby if things change.'

Harry saluted his sergeant, who strode away. Eve turned to Harry.

'Harry, what's—'

He put his arm in hers and walked her away from the rest of them. Storm clouds gathered overhead, turning the day to a dark, near-night. Once they were out of earshot of the others, he spoke.

'It's a dummy airfield,' he said, unable to look her in the eye. 'So the Nazis bomb here instead of a real one. We move lights around to make it look like planes are taking off.' He gestured to the large mesh baskets full of kindling. 'Then we set off the fire baskets to make them think they've hit us.' He sighed. 'We're decoys.'

'But you said you were a pilot. You said you were a captain . . .'

Harry looked away into the storm clouds. 'I was both of those things. Once. But after the crash, I . . .' He wiped the corner of an eye. 'Wind,' he said, shaking his head. 'After the crash, I . . . I couldn't fly. So they demoted me. Sent me here. Lack of moral fibre, they said. LMF. Means you're a coward. Officially.'

Neither spoke for a while. Eventually Eve broke the silence.

'Why didn't you tell me?' Her voice was small.

He tried to laugh. It sounded almost like a sob. 'I liked the way you saw me . . . Pathetic, isn't it . . .'

Eve slowly placed a hand on his cheek. She smiled at him. He pulled away.

'And there's that smile again,' he said. 'That enigmatic smile. Is that to patronise me?'

She shook her head and placed her hand on his cheek once more.

'No,' she said. 'It's not.'

He looked at her properly for the first time, and he saw what was in her eyes, just for him. She smiled once more. There was no mistaking the smile's meaning this time, and he returned it.

She kissed him and he kissed her back.

Friends Again?

The bunker had been cut into a hill. In other circumstances it would have been an exciting place to visit, a grand place for an adventure. But not today, not now. The children stood outside, huddled close to each other, not wanting to let anyone out of their sight.

All except one.

Edward stood slightly apart. He hadn't noticed what they had. He hadn't looked up when Mrs Hogg had followed the gruff sergeant inside the bunker, hadn't worried in case something happened to her and she never came out again. He hadn't watched Miss Parkins and the captain kissing and cuddling over by the fake planes.

He had just stood there, hands in pockets, lost in his thoughts, his sadness.

He became aware of whispers around him. For a few seconds he thought he was back in the house, hearing the old voices talking to him once more, but then he realised it was the other children, and they were talking about him. He tried hard to give the impression that he wasn't listening. He managed to catch snatches.

'Tom was mean to him . . .' Ruby's voice, her rough Cockney accent unmistakable, even at a low volume.

'And Joyce was going to tell . . .' Fraser. Edward didn't need to look to know that the little boy would be all wide-eyed as he spoke.

'And look what happened.' Ruby again. She had copied her mother's mannerisms, right down to the fact that if she made a statement and made it strongly enough, it was always right. 'Stands to reason, don't it?'

'Look.' James this time, getting angry. Trying to show leadership. 'Just . . . be quiet. All of you. Listen to what you're saying. This is stupid.'

The others fell silent. Edward relaxed slightly. He felt something warm inside for his former friend. Wished he could express it in some way.

'I think he did it.'

Edward froze. He knew that voice only too well. Flora. At times she had been his only ally, taking his side against the rest of them, standing up for him. Not any more.

He glanced up at her. She looked so sad and hurt. And something else, something even worse. She was scared of him, really, really terrified.

Edward longed to say something, longed even to cry. But he couldn't. Trapped in the prison of his own body, he just had to stand there while they all discussed him, pretending not to hear.

Ruby, emboldened by Flora's words, started up again. 'James,' she said, alarm in her voice, 'you spilled his milk.'

'No, I didn't,' said James, trying to shake off her words, but it was clear from his tone of voice that she was getting to him.

Ruby persisted. 'Yes, you did.'

'And . . . and . . . you locked him in a room, too.' Alfie was joining in now.

'That was Tom,' said James, exasperated. 'Not me.'

Edward saw Fraser raise his hand, point his finger at James, eyes still wide. 'You're next . . .'

'Oh, shut up, all of you,' said James. 'You're really, really pathetic. Childish.'

He turned away from them and walked over to join Edward, but Edward couldn't even look at him. He still felt the touch of that cold hand in his, even though they were miles away. Could still smell the chill and the rot of the house.

'Listen,' said James, once he was standing right next to him, 'I'm . . . sorry that we trapped you in the nursery. I didn't . . .' James sighed. 'I'm sorry. I did nothing. I should have done something and I didn't. And I'm sorry I spilled your milk, too. It was an accident, I didn't mean to.'

Edward said nothing. James moved round until he was directly in front of Edward and Edward couldn't look away.

'Can we be friends again?'

Edward wanted to answer, wanted to tell him, 'Yes, of course we can. Let's be friends, let's have fun together again. Like it used to be.'

But he couldn't.

He tried to, but that cold, dead hand tightened its grip on his, the smell of damp and rot growing even stronger. Edward had left the house, but the house was still within him.

'Edward?'

Edward just turned his head away, stared at the empty, flat horizon.

James, his eyes brimming with sadness, walked away.

It began to rain.

In the Bunker

The rain was coming down hard now, hitting the corrugated-metal roof like rapid machine-gun fire.

Eve had marshalled the children into the bunker as soon as the rain started. They were all there, huddled together in the middle of the room. Jean stood at the back of them, arms round the shoulders of the nearest ones, fingers digging into their flesh. Eve wasn't sure whether the headmistress was making sure they were safe, or whether the children were supporting her and keeping her upright.

The balance of power had shifted considerably within the group. Jean no longer had anything to offer, nothing constructive to contribute. What had happened was beyond her experience, beyond her comprehension. Eve had been put in charge. She didn't want that kind of leadership, but she hoped she was up to it. For all their sakes.

The bunker was windowless and depressing. It consisted mainly of a long room, the concrete walls covered with curved corrugated-metal sheets. The sheeting continued upwards, forming a ceiling. At one end was a ladder, leading to a hatch in the roof. At the other was a generator room from where the lighting, heating and incendiaries in the fire baskets were all controlled. Two overhead bulbs threw down a cheerless, sterile light into the room.

Eve looked at the children standing before her, wide-eyed and terrified. Even the Underground air-raid shelters would have been safer than this, she thought. She needed to find something to say that would comfort them, inspire them. Help them.

'Our train back to London is coming tomorrow,' she said. 'So we'll stay here tonight.'

She found her smile, put it in place. Looking at their scared and tired faces, it didn't seem to make much difference.

*

Harry opened a storecupboard in the generator room, pulled out some thin, padded mats.

'War Office issue, I'm afraid,' he said to Eve, who had followed him in, 'but they'll do for one night. The children can bed down on these.'

'Thank you.' Eve smiled. It was a different one from the smile that had failed to comfort the children. 'I'm sure they'll do fine.'

As Harry went about pulling out mats and counting them up, Eve had a look round. Her attention was immediately drawn to a battered old photograph propped on the control panel above the generator. She took it down. It showed an air crew standing in front of a bomber, all smiling, fresh-faced and full of life. She looked closer. Right in the middle was Harry.

'That's you, isn't it?' she asked, showing him the photo.

Harry looked up, his arms full of mats, ready to answer. Once he saw what she was holding, his expression darkened.

'It was,' he said.

He turned away from her, went on with his work.

✳

Night fell, bringing with it even more rain. The world became dark and full of static.

The children were still gathered together in the bunker. They had barely spoken, barely moved. Once Harry had unrolled the mats they had all bedded down on them. They were absolutely exhausted but too wired and scared to sleep. Instead they just lay there, the mats in a circle in the centre of the room. Like a western, thought Eve, all the wagons pulled round together to stop the Indians attacking.

Harry, Jean and Eve were sitting on folding metal chairs behind them. The only sound in the room was the incessant hammering of the rain on the roof.

Edward lay slightly apart from the others, hands clasped across his chest, staring at the ceiling. The other children were trying to sleep, or at least making a pretence of it. Edward was doing no such thing. It looked to Eve like the boy's body was a prison and he was trapped within it.

'Try to get some sleep,' she said.

As soon as she approached him, he flinched, turned away from her. He kept his eyes resolutely on the metal roof.

'It's all right, Edward. We're far away from the house. We're safe. She can't get you here.'

He didn't answer. She studied him. There was anger in his eyes. Anger at her? For what, throwing his Mr Punch doll back into the house? Was that it? Just as she opened her mouth to say something more, Ruby appeared at her side.

'Miss . . .'

'Yes, Ruby.'

'Tom told us Edward saw a ghost, Miss.'

The statement was so unexpected, it stopped Eve in her tracks. 'Well, I . . .'

'Did he?'

Eve's first response was to lie, to say that Tom had been talking nonsense. But she stopped herself. Ruby deserved more than that, more than lies. If they were ever to get away, if they were ever going to be safe, they all deserved more than lies.

'Yes, Ruby. He did. I saw her, too.'

'Eve . . .'

Eve looked up. Jean was shaking her head in admonishment. Eve ignored her, returned her attention to Ruby.

'Yes. I saw her, too. But it's all right. If she isn't

seen, then she can't hurt us. We're here now. We've left all that behind.'

Any pretence of sleep was gone. The rest of the children were listening now, all of them staring at Eve in fear and fascination, struggling to process the words, to cope with the information.

'Miss Parkins, stop this nonsense at once.'

Jean was staring at her, eyes blazing. She turned to the children. 'These are lies, children. Miss Parkins is trying to fill your head with rubbish and lies.'

'No,' said Harry. 'They aren't lies. Eve is telling the truth.'

Jean shook her head and sank back into her chair. But before she could come back with an argument, Harry spoke.

'I've had enough of lies,' he said. 'Enough of secrets. There are bad things out there. People that want to kill you, to kill all of us. These are dangerous times. And we don't get through dangerous times by ignoring them or pretending they're not happening. We get through them by working together. That's how we stop them.' He looked round at the group, then found Eve's hand and gave it a reassuring squeeze. 'All right?'

Eve smiled at him.

The children said nothing as they took in the information. Eventually Fraser, face screwed up in concentration, spoke.

'So, Miss, is the ghost Edward's mum, Miss?'

Eve shook her head. 'No, Fraser. This has nothing to do with—' She gestured over at Edward, about to say his name, but stopped dead.

In his hand was the Mr Punch doll. And from the way he was playing with it, it seemed to be talking to him.

Eve stared in horror. 'But I took that off you. We left it at the house . . .' She crossed over to him. 'Did she give it back to you?'

Edward ignored her. Just kept on playing with the doll.

'Tell me, Edward . . .'

He put the doll to his ear, listened, then nodded.

'Tell me!'

He didn't answer. Silence fell. Even the rain seemed quieter.

Then, in the distance, Eve heard a familiar song.

'Jennet Humfrye lost her baby . . .'

Harry stood up, looked round. He could hear it, too. 'What's that?'

'*Died on Sunday, seen on Monday . . .*'

The voices grew louder, echoing round the metal walls of the room. The children were all sitting up, fear etched on their faces.

All except Edward, who just lay there.

'*Who will die next? It must be YOU!*'

Eve's heart was hammering. 'She's here. Oh, God. She's here . . .'

Harry still held her hand. 'But nobody saw her. You said she only appears if . . .'

Eve looked down at Edward, still playing with the Mr Punch doll. 'She's come for Edward.'

Jean was on her feet. 'Now stop it. You're scaring the children.'

Eve turned to her. 'Did you not hear that?'

Jean stared back at her, ready to argue.

'You did, didn't you? What was it then? What were those voices?'

Jean's mouth opened and closed, but no words came out.

Before anyone else could speak or move, there came the sound of machinery rumbling into life from outside.

Harry ran into the generator room. The switches and dials on the control panel had come to life and turned themselves on.

'Someone's set the pyros off.'

'Pyros?' asked Eve.

'The fire baskets outside.'

He made to grab the controls, but before he could the board short-circuited and sparks flew out from it. Harry shielded his eyes. He reached out, tried the switches once more. Nothing responded.

'They won't turn off . . .'

In the main bunker, one of the overhead bulbs blew. The children screamed, hugged each other. The remaining bulb began to flicker and fizz.

The bunker was almost in darkness.

Around the walls, in the corners and the crevices, the shadows grew.

The Circle

Jean looked at Harry and Eve, standing by the control panel, talking to each other, deciding what to do next. Not even consulting her, pretending she was invisible. Or, worse, stupid.

'What do we do?' asked Eve.

Harry ran back into the room, having given up trying to alter any of the switches and dials by the generator. 'Stick together. That's the best thing we can do.'

Jean had had enough. 'Oh, please,' she said. 'You're being ridiculous. Quite ridiculous.' Her voice was becoming shrill and hysterical. She took a couple of breaths. 'Superstitious rubbish. It's just a . . . a fault. An electrical fault. We'll get out of this by being rational, not giving in to—'

'Everyone hold hands,' said Eve, ignoring Jean.

Eve and Harry moved the children into a circle. Eve made sure Edward was next to her, and took a firm hold of his hand.

'Right,' said Eve, trying to sound calm. 'We're all holding hands. If anyone lets go, two of us will know about it.'

Jean kept her hands at her side. 'Miss Parkins, this is—'

'Jean, please,' said Eve, cutting her off.

Jean felt anger rising within her. 'Don't be so—'

'Do it!' Harry shouted at her.

Jean, speechless and cowed by the authority in the young man's voice, meekly did as she was asked.

They stood in the circle. Unmoving, hardly breathing.

The ghostly nursery rhyme started up again.

'Jennet Humfrye lost her baby . . .'

The children all looked terrified. Eve wasn't letting herself feel the same way. Someone had to stay calm and rational, think of a way out. *Concentrate*, she thought, *ignore it and concentrate . . .*

'Jacob,' she said, thinking aloud. 'He was the only survivor . . . Blind . . . What did he say? He survived because he couldn't see her . . .' She looked round the rest of the group. 'That's it. Close your eyes. Everybody, close your eyes . . .'

'*Died on Sunday, seen on Monday . . .*'

'Now,' shouted Eve. 'Do it now . . .'

They all closed her eyes, even Jean. She felt ridiculous doing it, but something nagged at her, told her it was the right thing to do. Collective hysteria, she thought, going along with everyone else. But she didn't open her eyes.

'Miss,' said a voice that Jean identified as Fraser, 'Miss, I'm scared . . .'

Before Jean could answer, Eve said, 'It's all right, Fraser. Let's say our bedtime prayers. That'll help.'

'Don't let her get me . . . please . . .' James was sobbing.

Jean tried to open her mouth, speak, say something authoritative that would calm the situation down, but found that she had no words.

'Come on, everybody,' said Eve, 'all at once . . . "There are four . . ."'

'Who will die next? It must be YOU!'

'Come on,' said Eve, '"There are four corners . . ."'
The children joined in. '" . . . to my bed, four angels round my head . . ."'

'Jennet Humfrye lost her baby . . .'

'Louder,' said Eve.
The children chanted louder. '"One to watch and one to pray . . ."'

'Died on Sunday, seen on Monday . . .'

'"And two to bear my soul away . . ."'

'Who will die next? It must be YOU!'

Silence fell. No one dropped their hands or opened their eyes. The only sounds they could hear were the rain on the roof and the fire baskets igniting outside.

Jean tried not to listen to any of that. She just concentrated on her own breathing. Blackness and breathing. That was it. That's what would get her through this. Blackness and breathing.

Then she heard footsteps. Slow, measured footsteps.

'Don't let go, Edward . . .'

Eve. Jean thought that the boy must have dropped his hand, tried to get away. From the strength in Eve's voice, she wouldn't let him.

The footsteps were getting closer.

Blackness and breathing . . . Blackness and breathing . . . Jean screwed her already closed eyes even tighter.

'Don't look,' said Eve. 'Don't anyone open their eyes . . .'

Jean heard the footsteps slowly encircle the group. She desperately wanted to open her eyes, to see who was there. It was probably that gruff sergeant back again, ready to say something that would make them all feel ridiculous, make her feel stupid for joining in.

'This is ridiculous,' Jean said.

'Jean . . .' A warning in Eve's voice.

The footsteps still walking, still circling.

'No. I'm sorry, but this is . . .'

'Jean, don't. Please, don't . . .' Desperation in Eve's voice now.

The footsteps came to a halt.

'Madness,' said Jean.

She opened her eyes.

And there was the woman in black, her dead white face in Jean's, screaming right at her.

Pandemonium

Jean fell backwards, panicking, adding her screams to Jennet Humfrye's. As she fell she knocked into Eve, who, caught off balance, stumbled against one of the metal chairs, hitting her head as she fell to the floor. She lay motionless.

'Eve,' shouted Harry.

He rushed over to her and tried to pick her up. She lay there unresponsive, eyes closed.

The children screamed and ran, scattering into any available space in the semi-darkened room.

Harry looked round. Jennet seemed to have vanished once more, but that fact didn't seem to have calmed anyone down.

James had curled into a ball, hands over his head. He was sobbing, repeating the same phrase over and over again.

'Please don't punish me . . . please don't punish me . . .'

Harry saw Edward standing still, like the eye of a storm while chaos swirled around him. He lifted the Mr Punch doll to his ear once more, nodded, then ran towards the ladder.

'Edward! Wait!' The boy ignored him.

Harry looked down at Eve. She was breathing but unconscious. There was nothing he could do for her at the moment. He turned to Jean.

'Jean, look after the children. Keep them close.'

Jean didn't seem to have heard him. She sat in a corner, eyes wide and staring. Seeing nothing.

'Jean,' said Harry, sharply. 'The children . . .'

She nodded, numbly.

Harry gently placed Eve's head on the floor, stood up, and followed Edward up the ladder and out into the night.

The Shadow of a Child

Edward ran through the phantom airfield, as fast as his legs could go. The fake planes loomed, black birds of prey silhouetted against the dark grey storm-heavy night sky. The canvas flapping free in the wind and rain, slapping the wooden frames like the beating of large leathery wings. The shadows of huge, grotesque carrion crows following him wherever he went.

All around him the huge fire baskets caught and flared up, sending out vast blasts of light and heat; short, sharp bursts of intense illumination, sudden against the darkness, like ruptures from an exploding sun. And all the time, the rain poured down in near biblical torrents.

*

'Edward . . .'

Harry flung open the hatch and climbed out. He stood up, looked round. No sign of the boy. He was lost from view among the planes. Harry started running, searching.

A fire basket flared up and Harry, instead of shielding his eyes, used the sudden burst of light to scan the area.

There, up ahead, the shadow of a child through the canvas of a plane. Seen briefly, then gone.

Harry ran towards the plane.

No one there.

He looked round, trying to get his bearings, see which way Edward could have gone. Another burst from a fire basket, then another. Harry was disorientated, confused. He couldn't see Edward anywhere, couldn't see anything for a few seconds, apart from the after-image of the intense blast dancing on his retinas.

Harry waited for his sight to return to normal, then scanned the field again.

'Edward . . .'

There. He caught another glimpse of the running boy as he went behind one of the fake bombers. He gave chase and reached it, panting, head spinning from the explosions.

Another basket went up, the sudden flash illuminating the inside of the nearest bomber like an X-ray. And there he was. Inside the bomber, Harry saw — for a second or two — a child-sized shadow, huddled into the nose cone.

'Edward,' Harry shouted, 'it's all right . . . It's me, Harry . . . You're safe now . . .'

There was no reply. The light had disappeared and Harry couldn't see or hear anything from inside the plane. He walked round until he found the small maintenance hatch in the underside of the fuselage and pulled himself in.

Harry blinked. Again. And again. At first he thought the rain had blurred his vision, coming down so hard and fast outside, but inside the plane it was only trickling from leaks down the canvas seams. His head still spun from the proximity of the blasts, the rain exacerbating the pain by hammering down insistently on the plane's shell like nails against his skull. It was dark inside, darker than he had thought it would be.

He looked over to the nose cone where he had seen the shadow of the child, made his way slowly towards it.

'Edward . . .' He spoke softly so as not to alarm the boy. 'It's all right . . . you're safe now . . .'

Flames shot up outside, casting shadows against the canvas wall. The silhouette of a child appeared. Then another. And another. Then more, all seemingly standing outside the plane, waiting.

Harry blinked. *No*, he thought. *It's a trick of the light.* His eyes weren't yet accustomed to the sudden changes of light and dark.

And then he heard the singing.

'Jennet Humfrye lost her baby . . .'

Harry's head swam. 'Don't listen, Edward. Don't listen . . .'

More silhouettes appeared on the other side of the plane, lit by flashes of light. The singing became louder.

'Died on Sunday, seen on Monday . . .'

'Don't listen to them . . .' Harry shouted. 'Don't give in to them . . .'

The voices became louder still.

'Who will be next? It must be YOU!'

Then silence. The shadows disappeared. The singing stopped. All Harry could hear was the hammering of his heart, the pumping of blood in his ears. He breathed a sigh of relief.

'It's all right, Edward,' he said. 'They've gone. We're safe. Now, give me your hand . . .'

Harry reached out, touched the shoulder of the boy, tried to turn him round.

It wasn't a boy.

The corpse, waterlogged, bloated and decayed, stared at Harry with its one remaining eye.

'Help me, Captain, help me . . .'

The Fire Basket

Harry screamed and jumped away from the appar-
ition, landing on his back. He couldn't breathe; his
chest had a tightening steel band wrapped round
it.

The corpse had gone. In its place were only a
bundle of unpainted canvas and half-empty tins of
paint.

Still shaking, he looked round. He was alone.

He got out of the plane as quickly as he could.

Edward was still running. He no longer knew where
to or what from, all he knew was that he must keep
running.

The perimeter fence stopped him getting too far. He had crashed into it at one point and turned round to go in the other direction. That route had led to the hill that he was now running up. He hoped there was a way out on the other side.

A fire basket went off. He found himself exposed on the hill's ridge, silhouetted against the night sky.

'Edward!'

Harry was sprinting towards him.

No, he thought. *Have to get away, got to keep going . . .*

He ran on, over the crest of the hill, down the other side. He turned round to see that Harry was gaining on him.

Then he lost his footing on the wet grass, slipped and went tumbling down the hill.

Edward didn't know where he was. He couldn't see anything. His glasses were gone, knocked off in the fall.

He felt around him, squinted. He was lying on a bed of wood, and he could smell oil. He sat up, felt wire mesh by his fingertips.

He could just about make out the rise of the hill above him and quickly worked out where he was.

He had fallen into a fire basket.

He got to his knees, desperately trying to scramble out of it before it ignited.

Harry saw him fall, saw him land in the basket.

'Edward . . .'

He ran even faster, ignoring the tiredness in his body, pushing himself on. He had to get to Edward before—

Harry was thrown backwards as the fire basket exploded.

This Is Your Fault . . .

Eve opened her eyes. Abstract, blurred images coalesced, began to form into something solid, corporeal and sharply defined. Muffled, distorted sounds became correctly pitched and distinct. She made out a face looking down at her, a worried, concerned expression.

'Harry?'

She sat up, looked round, her head throbbing as she did so. Made out the dimly lit concrete and corrugated metal of the bunker, heard the incessant drumming of the rain. Everything looked grey and washed out. Or perhaps that was just how she felt.

Eve saw the children and Jean huddled together.

They all looked terrified. The way the older woman clung to them, it was hard to see who was comforting whom.

Eve rubbed her head. It hurt. 'How long have I . . . ?'

'A couple of hours,' said Harry.

Eve looked round once more, urgently, ignoring the pain in her head this time.

'Where's Edward?'

Harry was holding something in his hand. He opened his fingers, let Eve see what was there. In the palm of his hand, all singed and twisted, the lenses shattered, were Edward's glasses.

Eve shook her head, increasing the pain, but she didn't care. 'No . . . no, no, no . . .'

'He ran. I chased after him. He . . . fell into a fire basket, I . . .' Harry's voice wavered. 'I couldn't reach him before it . . . I tried . . . I'm sorry, I'm so, so sorry . . .'

Eve didn't know what to say, what to do. Anger and sadness welled up within her, fought for prominence. She grimaced, fingers flexing into fists. She needed an outlet. Turned to Jean.

'You let go,' she said.

Jean just stared, open-mouthed. 'I . . .'

Eve stabbed a finger at her. 'This is your fault . . .'

Jean put her head down and began to cry. 'I'm sorry . . .'

'Eve.' Harry took hold of Eve's shoulders. 'Stop it. Yes, I'm sure you want somebody to blame. If that's the case, blame Jennet. This is nobody's fault but hers.'

Eve's shoulders slumped and the fight went out of her. The only sounds in the room were the rain and Jean's sobbing.

Eve frowned as a sudden thought struck her. 'It doesn't make sense.'

She shrugged off Harry's grip, went over to Edward's few belongings and began searching through them.

'What are you doing, Eve?' asked Harry.

She was rummaging through Edward's bag.

'His drawing . . . He wouldn't have . . . Here it is.'

Eve drew it out, looked at it. It had changed. The boy and the woman were now standing in front of a house. The woman's clothes were floor length and heavily coloured in with black. A veil covered her face. The boy was holding something in his hands. The Mr Punch doll. Eve smiled at Harry, a wild, desperate look of vindication in her eyes.

'Edward's still alive,' she said.

'Eve,' Harry said, not unkindly, 'you're in shock.'

'No,' she said, her voice calm and low. 'No, I'm not. Did you see his body?'

'He was in there. I saw him fall, I . . .'

'Did you see his body?'

Harry made a helpless gesture. 'There was nothing left to see . . .'

They stopped talking as they heard the sound of an approaching vehicle. It pulled up outside the bunker.

'She's taken him back to the house,' said Eve. She held up Edward's drawing and was about to explain further when the hatch was pulled back and Jim Rhodes let himself in.

'Captain Burstow,' he said, once he had made his way down the ladder, 'why the hell did you bring all these children here?'

Eve didn't have the time or the energy to waste on arguing with Jim Rhodes. Her only thought was to get back to the house and save Edward.

'They couldn't stay in the house any longer,' said Harry. 'It wasn't safe.'

'Safe? What d'you mean?' He turned to face Eve. 'Was this your idea, Miss Parkins? Some kind of nonsense?'

But it was Jean who answered him. She stood up, walked right up to him. Her face was tear-streaked, her hair dishevelled, clothing crumpled. There was barely any trace of the previously fastidious woman who had absolute belief in her own authority. Instead there was hurt, damage and rage.

'Three children, Dr Rhodes. Three children. Look. Look for yourself. They've gone. Dead. Dead, because of that house, of what's . . . what's in that house . . .'

Jim Rhodes just stared at her.

'I told you,' Jean went on. 'I told you that place wasn't safe, but would you listen? Oh, no. You left us there. And now this. This . . .' The tears were falling down her cheeks now. 'Why? Why would you do that? Why . . . ?'

She broke down into sobs once more, her hands covering her face.

'Jean . . .' Harry placed a protective arm round her shoulders.

Jim Rhodes just stared at her. 'I did . . . I did what I thought I . . .'

No one noticed Eve climb the ladder and leave the bunker.

Back to the Old House

Eve climbed out of the hatch and ran across the tarmac towards the Jeep. She heard Harry calling after her. She didn't have time to stop for him, she had only one thought.

Get back to the house and save Edward.

She drove away from the airfield, the image of Harry's forlorn figure diminishing in the side mirror, and felt a pang of emotion for him. She didn't like leaving him behind, or being without him. She had grown to care about him. She hoped that, once this was all over, he might stay around.

Once this was all over.

If this was ever over.

She drove through the wind and rain, the Jeep's wipers failing to keep pace with what the storm threw at the windscreen, and tried to calm herself, think logically, rationally. She had to be strong when she got back to the house. Brave. There was no room for emotions, for confusion in her mind. Edward was in there, she was sure of it. And Jennet mustn't claim him.

She left the mainland and crossed over Nine Lives Causeway, the mist rolling in from the sea, shrouding the Jeep as she went. Waves washed up to the sides of the road, crashed over on to the causeway. The tide was coming in. Eve felt that the whole world was drowning. That everything was conspiring against her, trying to stop her reaching Eel Marsh Island.

But still she drove on.

Eel Marsh House looked even more desolate and ruined than when Eve had first seen it. The vines and weeds had returned; overgrowing the gardens once more in the short time she had been away, as if they had never been cut back. The house and grounds were reverting to how Jennet wanted them, she thought.

Eve parked the Jeep before the gates, got out and pushed them open. They were heavy, rusted and old. Closed since she had last been here. They put up resistance, only opening with a screech of corroded metal on metal, and under much duress, seemingly reluctant to let her in.

Beyond the gates the house, battered by the wind and rain pelting down on it, looked like it was fighting to stay upright, not to be dragged down into the ground or claimed by the surrounding water.

There were no lights at the windows. It seemed empty.

But Eve knew better.

Taking a deep breath, then another, trying to calm her wildly beating heart, she walked up towards the front door.

The House Diseased

Eve pushed open the huge old door. The house was dark except for narrow shafts of moonlight creeping round the corners of the blackout blinds and curtains. She stood still, listened. The only sound she could hear was rainwater, pouring in through the leaks in the house. Nothing else. No one else.

'Edward?'

No reply. She tried the light switch, fearing the water might short it out. The bulbs came slowly, reluctantly, to life. Or half life; they fizzed and buzzed, radiating erratically, never becoming fully bright.

The struggling lights weakly illuminated the

hallway. Eve gasped at what she saw. The blackness had spread. The whole house was damp and decrepit, mould and rot feasting on the building like a cancerous, corrupting disease.

Eve couldn't see her, but she could feel her. Jennet. Everywhere. The rot, the corruption, was just the outward manifestation, a demonstration that her hold on the house was now virtually complete.

Eve went into the children's dormitory. The beds were as they had left them, unmade and unkempt. Except for one: Joyce's. Her little body lay there, a sheet covering it, her gas mask on the floor where Harry had thrown it. They hadn't known what to do with her body, so had left it to be dealt with the next day. Eve looked at it and felt sadness and helplessness begin to take her over.

No. She wouldn't give in. Joyce's body was a reminder of what had happened. It was also a warning not to let things go any further. Jennet must not win. Eve wasn't going to let her.

She couldn't look at the dead little girl any longer and turned away, leaving the room.

Back in the hallway, she called again.

'Edward?'

Silence, but for the rain.

Doubt rose up in her. Maybe she was wrong. Maybe he had died at the airfield and this was all a—

Creak . . . crack . . .

Her stomach flipped; her heart skipped a beat. The sound came again.

Creak . . . crack . . . Creak . . . crack . . .

The same rhythmic noise that she had heard during her first night in the house. The one that had got her out of bed and down into the cellar. The one that had started all of this.

Creak . . . crack . . . Creak . . . crack . . .

It wasn't coming from the cellar this time. She listened again, harder. It was coming from upstairs.

Eve felt her heart palpitating. She looked round, listened once more.

Creak . . . crack . . . Creak . . . crack . . .

It was definitely coming from upstairs. And, she thought with a feeling of dread, she could guess which room, too. She took a few seconds, composed herself. And began to climb the stairs.

Water ran down the walls, pooling on the stairs. The wood was in a terrible state, rotten and soaked. When she pressed her foot down, water oozed out from either side. She felt the treads warp and bend beneath her as she placed her weight on them. They seemed to shriek in pain when she touched them. She kept going, using Harry's lighter to guide the way.

Creak . . . crack . . . Creak . . . crack . . .

She reached the landing, began to walk down the hallway. The wall lights were even dimmer up here, throwing just the ghost of an illumination on to the walls, making the shadows dance with imagined horrors. The ill-lit meandering trickles of rainwater were like veins and arteries against the rotted walls.

Creak . . . crack . . . Creak . . . crack . . .

The sound was loudest behind the nursery door. Eve held the lighter out before her, walking towards it, fearing something would appear from the shadows before she reached it.

She stopped in front of the door. It was closed, but the noise was definitely coming from within.

Creak . . . crack . . . Creak . . . crack . . .

She reached for the handle, turned it. The door swung open.

Eve stood on the threshold, not daring to enter, not daring to look at what was inside, but she couldn't just walk away. She had come too far, lost too much. It had to end. Now.

She closed her eyes.

Creak . . . crack . . . Creak . . . crack . . .

Tried to ignore the voice in her head that was screaming at her to run away, to turn back, the trembling in her legs and arms, the hammering of her heart.

She took a deep breath. Another.

And stepped inside the room.

The Nursery Regained

The nursery was transformed.

The carpet was thick and rich, the curtains heavy and brocaded. A large, ornate wooden wardrobe dominated a corner of the room. Oil lamps on the papered walls gave out a warm, comforting glow. Against one wall was a child's bed, and toys were strewn all over the floor. Cymbal-clashing monkeys, red-tunicked soldiers, a spinning top and a candy-striped Punch and Judy theatre.

There was no damp here, no decay.

Edward sat in the centre of the floor, playing intently. He had his back to Eve and didn't turn as she entered. She noticed that he was dressed differently, like the boy from the photograph. Eve saw what the focus of his attention was. Mr Punch. No longer as decayed or decrepit as the rest of the house, the puppet looked brand new, its painted-on grin viciously triumphant.

Creak . . . crack . . . Creak . . . crack . . .

The rocking chair was next to him, swinging backwards and forwards. It was the same one Eve had seen in the cellar, the one she suspected had made the noise the first night she was in the house. Like the room, it had also been restored. There was no one in it, but it didn't stop moving.

Eve pocketed Harry's lighter and slowly approached Edward.

'Edward . . .'

He didn't move. Didn't turn round, didn't look up. He gave no indication that he had heard her, just sat there playing with that leering wooden puppet.

'Edward . . .' she repeated, louder.

She extended her hand, touched him on the shoulder.

Edward turned quickly, a ferocious look in his eyes. He lashed out with Mr Punch, catching Eve in the face.

Eve staggered back, her hand to her cheek, feeling blood there. Edward had returned to his toy, his back to Eve once more. Sitting calmly, as if nothing had happened.

Creak . . . crack . . . Creak . . . crack . . .

Eve thought of turning round, walking out of the room, the house. But she stopped herself. No. She wouldn't let Jennet win.

'Edward.'

She walked back up to him. To prevent him from lashing out again, she pinned his arms down by his sides. He struggled, trying to shake himself free, squirming to be rid of her, but she wouldn't let go. He still clung on to Mr Punch. Eve clung on to Edward.

'Edward . . . we need to leave . . .'

She moved towards the door, the wriggling boy held firmly in her grasp.

As she reached the door, the rocking chair stopped moving.

A shudder passed through Eve. Adrenalin pumped hard round her system. Grabbing the struggling Edward as tightly as she could, she managed to run through the door just before it slammed shut.

Once outside the nursery, Eve didn't look back. Didn't dare to see who or what was following her. She ran for the stairs, Edward struggling in her arms, trying desperately to free himself from her grasp, make his way back to the room. His features were feral, lips drawn back over his teeth. As she ran he swiped at her face, fingers hard and curled into talons, raking her skin and drawing blood. The pain seared across her face, but she refused to slow down or let go of the boy. He began hitting her with the Mr Punch doll. She tried to ignore it, concentrate on getting the boy out of the house.

The black mould spread out from the nursery door, the walls cracking at its touch, pursuing them down the hallway, trying to ensnare them.

The creeping darkness caught up with Eve. She glanced to her side, saw it. Pushed herself to run faster.

She reached the stairs and hurried down them as fast as she could, desperate not to lose her footing or to let go of Edward.

A high-pitched shrieking reverberated round the walls, lapped in a storm of fury. Eve ignored it, kept running.

The mould was spreading fast now, sinking into the walls as it went, forcing them to crumble, break apart. Part of the wall next to Eve fell in, showering her with plaster. She grabbed the bannister to steady herself, gasping, forcing damp dust from her mouth and eyes. As she did, she almost dropped Edward, but managed to shift her weight so that she still kept moving forward.

The front door was right ahead of her. Her spirits rose at the thought of it. All she had to do was reach the bottom of the stairs, run across the hallway and get out. A matter of seconds. That was all.

She didn't notice the black decay pass her, slide up the remaining stairs before her, claiming the already rotted wood. But she noticed them collapse.

Eve saw what had happened, but her momentum was too great. She couldn't stop. She tripped and fell, landing flat on the floor. As she did so, she loosed her grip on Edward and the boy managed to break free.

'No . . .'

He bolted from her, into the shadows. Eve was straight back on her feet, determined not to let him get away. She saw him run into the corner of the hallway, the inky blackness ready to enfold him, swallow him up. She threw herself at him, arms outstretched, a last, desperate move. If he evaded her grasp, she would lose him for ever.

Her hands connected. He stopped moving. Her impetus carried her onwards. She landed on top of him. Smiled. She had him.

Then the floor gave way and they fell into the darkness.

Demons of the Mind

Harry put his head down, concentrated on the steering wheel, the road ahead, the rain beyond. Nothing more.

He tried to ignore the rising tide that was smashing against the wheels of the bus as he drove over the causeway. Block his ears to the screams of the drowning that he was sure he could hear being carried on the wind.

When Eve had driven away in his Jeep, he hadn't stopped to think. Jim Rhodes's bus was standing idling and Harry had jumped in it, driven straight off. He knew where Eve was headed. He just hoped he would be in time to help her.

The waves crashed harder against the bus, building in size and ferocity. The screams of the drowning intensified.

'No . . . no . . .'

He tried his usual trick, hammering on the steering wheel three times. It didn't change anything. Sweat beading his brow, hands shaking, he drove on. Determined not to give in, not to let Eve down.

And then he heard the voice.

'*Help us, Captain . . . help us . . .*'

'No, no, no, no . . .'

Harry drove even faster.

'*Help us . . .*'

Harry became aware that he wasn't alone. He risked a sideways glance. There sat the drowned airman he had seen in the fake plane. His uniform soaked and rotten, his face eaten away, one eye missing, reaching out to him.

'*Help us . . .*'

Harry, heart hammering, kept his eyes on the road ahead.

He heard movement behind him, from the aisle of the bus. Someone changing seats, moving forward. Then another. And another. Slow, shuffling. Dragging as they came; heavy, waterlogged.

He glanced in his rear-view mirror, became aware of shadows, lumpen, misshapen, moving about.

'*Help us . . .*'

'You're not real,' Harry shouted. 'All of you . . . Any of you . . .'

'*You killed us . . .*'

'No, I didn't! I didn't . . .' Harry screamed. The bus lurched to the left, perilously close to the edge of the water. He managed to wrestle it back on to the road just in time.

'No,' he said, 'I didn't kill you. We were hit . . . I tried to save you . . .'

Silence from the bus.

Harry kept talking, kept his eyes ahead. 'You're not real. You're ghosts. I carry you everywhere I go. But you're not real. You're just my guilt. That's all. Because I couldn't save you. I tried and I . . . I couldn't.'

Nothing.

'And I'm . . . sorry. I'll always be sorry. I did what I could. And I failed. And I'll always carry that with me. I'll always carry you with me.'

He risked a glance at his side. The ghosts had disappeared. Harry was alone.

It was the first time he had acknowledged how

he felt about what had happened and his failure to save his crew. Out loud. To himself. He felt a calmness wash over him. Strength ran through his body. He was properly alone. For the first time in a long time, he had no one with him.

He put his head down, concentrated once more on the road ahead, the rain beyond.

Jennet Triumphant

The water stank, tasted of stagnation and corruption, like rancid dead fish and more besides. It filled Eve's nostrils and mouth, making her cough and gag. She couldn't spit it out quick enough. She put her feet on the ground.

She and Edward were in the cellar. The wooden shelves had splintered and smashed, as the floor had given way, and they had fallen into them, the boxes upended, the contents now floating all about. The water was high, impossibly so, Eve thought. Much higher than it had been before, at waist height. Overhead pipes had burst, spraying their brackish contents all over her. The water gushed through the airbricks. The walls were crumbling, the resistance in the stone weakening as the water from outside poured in, getting faster, threatening to tear out the house's foundations.

The fizzing, faltering light bulbs cast weak, intermittent illumination.

Eve hurt all over, but she didn't have time to check herself. She had to find Edward. She saw him, standing at the top of the steps, the doll clutched to his chest.

Standing next to him was Jennet Humfrye. Their pose was exactly like that of Edward's drawing, and the photograph, the walls blackening and crumbling all around them.

'Edward,' she shouted above the noise of the water, 'Edward . . . are you all right?'

He didn't reply.

She made to move towards him but found that her legs were held fast. She looked down. Silver grey coils moved about her ankles, weighing her down, stopping her moving. Nipping and biting at her legs. Living, writhing chains.

Eels.

Eve swallowed back the urge to scream.

'Edward . . .'

The boy just stared down at her.

'Edward, you have to help me . . .'

Edward kept staring. Eve saw his expression. Like he was in a trance. Jennet inclined her head. He looked up at her, his head on one side as if listening, receiving instructions. Then he nodded.

'Edward, no . . .'

Edward began to walk down the steps. Slowly, ignoring the rapidly rising water.

'No,' shouted Eve, trying desperately to pull her legs free. 'No . . . you can't have him . . . No . . .'

Edward clutched Mr Punch tightly to his chest as he descended into the water. He walked into the centre of the cellar, out of Eve's reach. Stopped moving. Eve realised what he was going to do, what Jennet was willing him to do. Drown himself.

The water level kept rising. It bobbed and splashed, covering Edward's mouth. He made no attempt to walk or swim away, just stared straight ahead.

'Wake up . . . Edward, please, wake up . . .'

Eve struggled to free herself from the coils of eels, but they just gripped her legs tighter. She opened her mouth as wide as she could, found a voice as loud as she could manage.

'He's not yours . . .' she shouted at the figure at the top of the stairs.

Her only answer was a loud rumbling and cracking as the whole house started to shake, decay spreading everywhere.

'Leave him alone . . .'

Eve looked over at Edward once more. The water was almost covering his nose now. His eyes were still open. Eve thought she saw the struggle going on inside him, behind those eyes. She didn't know if it was just her imagination, the flickering illumination making her see things that weren't there, but she had to believe it, had to cling on to it. He was in there. And he was fighting to get out.

'Edward,' she shouted, 'you have to fight her, you have to . . . don't give in to her . . .'

The water covered Edward's nose. He stopped trying to breathe.

'Edward . . .' Eve thought frantically. 'You . . . you fight bad dreams with good thoughts . . . Remember?' No response. Edward closed his eyes. Eve's voice became even louder. 'Edward, you fight bad dreams with good thoughts. Your mother told you that. Remember? Your mother . . .'

Edward opened his eyes and looked to the top

of the steps. Jennet was gone. In her place stood Edward's mother, resplendent in her good black coat, standing just as he had last seen her, in the doorway of their house, calling to him, reaching out to him, a shimmering, impossible image.

The wall cracked around her, just as it had done in the explosion. And she was gone.

In her place was Jennet.

Edward closed his eyes once more and put his head under water.

'No . . . No . . .' Eve's voice was a small, defeated thing. She had no fight left in her. She had failed.

Edward was gone. Jennet was triumphant.

The Ghost Choir

Eve stared at where Edward's head had disappeared. There was nothing to mark his passing, not even any air bubbles. She just had to accept that he had drowned. She felt that pain like a knife in her heart.

Then, as she watched, the water began to roil and bubble and Edward appeared once more. He threw his head back, gasping for air. His arms came up and he flung the Mr Punch doll as hard as he could towards the steps.

A terrifying scream echoed round the room.

A thrill of hope ran through Eve. 'You've lost,' she shouted to the walls. 'He's rejected you . . .'

Huge splits sundered the walls, like lightning bolts running up and over the ceiling. Jennet's rage was tearing the house apart.

The eels loosened their grip on Eve's legs, and she managed to pull herself free of them. The water was up to her neck now, and she struggled to half-swim, half-walk towards where Edward was treading water. The boy held out his hands, his face showing relief and happiness at seeing her. Eve felt something within her break.

She reached him.

'You're safe now . . . I've got you . . .'

As she spoke, hands appeared from beneath the water. Small, grey, emaciated. Children's hands, but grasping and clawed. They grabbed Edward, began to pull him down.

'No . . .'

Eve tried to pull the boy back towards her, make their way to the few stairs that were still above water, but more hands appeared, tugging and clutching. They were on her, too, grabbing her clothes, her limbs, pulling her down with him.

'Let us go . . .'

There were too many to fight. The hands pulled them both under the water.

Once she had been dragged under, Eve opened her eyes.

Through the murky water, she could see that the cellar floor had given way, the walls were following. The outside was coming inside. All around her and Edward were small, writhing shapes. Jennet's victims. The ghost choir. Still marked by the manners of their deaths, their burns, mutilations and poisonings. No longer human, now just ravaged wraiths. Dead fish eyes and sleek fish skin, jaws distending, displaying mouths of pointed, sharp teeth, hands fin-sharp and claw-like.

Grabbing at Eve and Edward, pulling them down to the sudden depths.

Eve, air rapidly running out, fought them as hard as she could, forcing the fingers off her body, pulling away from their sickening embrace. Edward was doing the same, frantically scrabbling to be free.

Eve looked upwards, saw Jennet standing above the water, returned to the steps of the cellar, malignantly exultant. Eve renewed her efforts to escape, but the hands were too strong, too many. Digging into her clothes, her flesh. Pulling her relentlessly down.

Edward stopped struggling, clung hard to her. Eve, sensing the futility of fighting further, accepted what was to happen and hugged him tightly. She could feel his little body trembling.

They would be together for the last few seconds of life and then slip away.

Eve closed her eyes.

The Fall

Harry parked the bus, the wind and rain soaking him almost instantly, and ran straight into the house. It was crumbling, falling down around him. He looked round the hallway, saw the hole in the floor, the water rising right up to it. The house was rotting from the inside out.

'Eve . . .'

No reply. He looked again at the hole in the floor. The water was almost up to the ceiling. Then he heard screams coming from down there. A woman's voice. Eve.

He pulled off his greatcoat, ready to jump straight in. But something stopped him. The hole

was small; there were too many unknown factors.
Instead he ran through to the kitchen, pulled open
the door to the cellar.

There stood Jennet.

She turned her baleful, malevolent eyes on him.
Moved towards him.

'Don't,' he said.

She stopped.

'I'm not scared of you,' he said, feeling calmer
and more confident than he had for a long while.
'You've got no power over me any more.'

She stared at him.

'You could have done more for Nathaniel. It's
not just your own rage at what was done to you. It's
your guilt that you didn't do enough for him.'

Something flickered behind Jennet's obsidian eyes.

'Now move.' He jabbed his finger at her.

She flinched and moved aside.

The steps were nearly submerged by the rising
water. He saw the faint outline of two figures being
dragged away from the surface, down into the
depths, and dived straight in.

Eve looked up and saw him. His presence re-
energised her and she began to pull at the claws
with renewed vigour.

Harry swam towards them, grabbing hold of Edward. The boy resisted at first, thinking it was another of Jennet's attacks, but with Eve's encouragement allowed Harry to take him away.

As Harry grasped Edward, the ghost choir loosed their grip, cowering away from him in fear. Harry took Eve's hand and pulled her up with him. Her heart was pounding, adrenalin and hope hammering round her body as the three of them moved up to the surface.

Then a hand reached out, grabbed Eve's necklace, pulling her whole body backwards once more, dragging her down again.

She let go of Harry, put her hand to her throat, wrenching away from the grasp, trying not to choke. As she did so, more hands appeared, clutching at her.

The necklace snapped. The cherub pendant sank slowly down and away.

Eve made to dive down after it, but Harry grabbed her, pulled her back to the surface.

Let it go, she thought. *Keep moving forward.*

They broke the surface at the same time, gasping for air.

'Come on,' shouted Harry, swimming over towards the stairs.

With a groan, the ceiling above the stairs col-
lapsed, blocking their escape.

'Jennet . . .' managed Eve, flinching from falling
masonry. She looked around. 'This way . . .'

Eve began swimming towards the other end of
the cellar, to the hole she and Edward had fallen
through. Harry followed, Edward on his back.
The water had almost reached the cellar ceiling
as Harry lifted Edward up and helped him to
scramble through the opening above them. Once
the boy was out of the way, he turned to Eve.

'Your turn,' he said, helping her up.

Eve pulled herself up on to the hallway floor,
free of the water, still gasping for air. Around her,
the house was quivering and shaking. Timber and
stone debris were littered about the place, and she
had to jump out of the way as another roof beam
came down near her.

'Quickly,' she said, stretching out her hand to
help Harry out of the water.

He clutched her hand, began to pull himself up.
His eyes caught hers. He smiled. She returned it.

Then he caught sight of something else behind
her, and his expression changed.

Jennet was standing in the corner of the hallway,

staring at them. She looked up at the ceiling, screamed with rage.

Harry realised what was about to happen, what she was doing. He got to his feet and, instinctively, grabbed hold of Edward and Eve and pushed them out of the way towards the front door.

Eve, thrown off balance, landed on the floor. She looked up. Saw the ceiling above Harry collapse on top of him.

'Harry!'

She watched his body slacken and crumple as the weight of the wood and stone knocked him unconscious, breaking his bones, crushing him. The floorboards beneath him splintered from the force, and Harry's now lifeless body was taken into the rising water which surged and splashed all over the hallway.

Jennet kept screaming. The walls shook and crumbled; the rest of the ceiling was about to give way. One last attempt by Jennet to claim Edward.

Eve pushed the boy through the door and followed him out.

The screams intensified. The glass of the windows shattered, Jennet's rage reflected in every shard.

Eve and Edward ran stumbling from the house, not daring to stop, to look back. They skidded and rolled down the driveway, coming to a stop past the gates before the causeway. Eve turned, looked back at the house.

All that remained was a blackened, rotted shell surrounded by rubble. Jagged walls, twisted beams and, oozing from the centre, a deep pool of black water spilled out like an oil slick.

The screams had echoed away to nothing.

Silence.

'Harry . . .'

Eve knew he was gone, but she couldn't bring herself to admit it. Tears streamed down her face. She screamed and sobbed his name.

'Harry . . .'

She sat unmoving, staring at the carcass of the house.

Then a small hand slowly took her own. Squeezed. She looked down. Edward.

'I'm sorry . . .'

The first words he had spoken.

Eve put her arms round him. Held him as tightly as she could. His tears joined hers.

The rain stopped. Dawn began to break.

A cold, distant sun broke through the mist and shone down on them.

Many Happy Returns

The Blitz was over and London, or most of it, was still standing.

The roads were strewn with rubble. Nearly every street was marred by ruined buildings, like the remains of an ancient civilisation waiting for the new, modern one to emerge from it. The past was over. The future still to be written.

The heavy pall of fear had lifted from the city. Now Londoners went about their daily lives without the fear of imminent death. The commonplace terror of going to sleep and dreading not waking was gone. The panic of Nazi invasion had abated. For now. The war still rumbled on, but it was, for the most part, a distant thing. People were pulling together, making an effort. For the first time in a long while, they dared to hope.

In the parlour of her small, tidy, terraced house in Hackney, Eve Parkins was putting the finishing touches to a birthday present she was wrapping. The summer sun streamed in through the windows, making it the kind of day that anyone would feel grateful to live through. That was how Eve was trying to feel. And, for the most part, succeeding.

She carried the brightly wrapped parcel into the living room. Edward stood there in his best clothes, looking in the mirror, trying to straighten his tie.

'Ready?' she said to him.

He turned to her. 'Yes.'

Eve straightened his collar, pushed his tie into place. 'Very smart.'

He smiled at her and Eve felt her heart break.

Seven months. That was how long it had been since the events at Eel Marsh House. Seven months of pain and anger and sadness, of guilt and loss, recrimination and rebuilding. And finally, mercifully, the relief they had felt coming from just being alive. Eve and Edward had started a new life together. They had left the house. She just hoped the house could leave them.

'Here,' she said, handing him the present. 'Happy birthday.'

Edward smiled. Joyfully, naturally. Eve felt a painful kind of love for him in that moment. He started to unwrap his present, Eve helping him. He pulled off the paper to reveal a new set of coloured pencils and a big book of sketch paper.

'So you can make new drawings,' she said. 'Colourful ones.'

Edward looked at the sketchbook. Eve saw his smile fade away, and his expression alter. Like clouds obscuring the sun on a summer's day. He was the mute boy again. Eve's heart skipped a beat.

'Edward? What's wrong?'

He kept staring at the pencils. Eventually he looked up.

'Will she come back?'

It never left them. No matter how far away they had moved, how much they had tried to fill their lives together with other things, it was always there. *She* was always there. They would be out somewhere, in a park or on the street, and one of them would catch a glimpse of someone who looked like her, and they would be plunged back to that night in the house once more. Then the moment would pass and life would slowly begin again. These little interludes had become less and less frequent as time wore on, and Eve hoped that eventually they would disappear altogether. The sharp pain would become a dull ache. It would happen and it was happening. But not quite yet.

'Will she?' Edward asked, his eyes fearful.

'No,' said Eve. 'She's gone.'

Edward kept staring at her, seeking reassurance. Eve said the words she had spoken so many times to him, the words he needed to hear, to believe in. The words that she wanted to believe in, too.

'She fed on all the bad feelings inside of us. So if we stay happy, she can't come back. Do you understand? You have to promise me you'll be happy. All right?'

'Yes . . .' Edward didn't sound so sure.

'Edward?'

'Yes.' Firmer this time.

'Good. Now where's my smile?'

Edward smiled. And the sun-filled room became so much brighter.

'Very good,' she said.

'Your turn,' said Edward, still smiling.

Eve pointed to the corners of her mouth and slowly formed a smile for him. It wasn't like her smile of old, part of her daily battle armour; it was something different, something new. A smile born out of joy and relief and love for Edward. Edward knew that, and it made him love her even more for it.

But her smile faltered as she glanced at the framed photo on the wall. It did that, caught her off guard. Even the sunniest days could cast the darkest shadows.

Unexpected tears formed in the corners of her eyes as she became lost in the photograph and her memories. Harry and his crew. All looking at the camera, all smiling. Forever smiling. She had rescued it from the fake airfield, taken it home and framed it. It was all she had of Harry. The bravest man she had ever met.

She wiped her eyes. Remembered what he had said about living in the present, about being there for the people who need you now.

'Come on, you. Time to go.' She took Edward's hand and they left the house, walking off down the street.

The living room was left empty.

Almost empty.

A figure stepped forward from shadow to sunlight and stared at the framed photograph. At the smiling faces.

Other figures stepped forward too. Small, emaciated figures, their bodies showing the manner of their deaths, their eyes empty. Their mouths opened and they began their whispered, hushed singing once more.

'*Jennet Humfrye lost her baby . . . Died on Sunday, seen on Monday . . . Who will die next? It must be YOU . . .*'

The ghost choir dispersed. The tall, dark figure stared at the photograph until the glass cracked. Her bone-white face reflected back at her in dozens of jagged slivers.

She melted slowly back into the shadows.

And waited.

My relationship with Hammer

Children of the Stones. Sky. King of the Castle. Ace of Wands. Timeslip. The Changes. Public information films with a Donald Pleasance voiceover. And of course, *Doctor Who.* The Seventies was a fine decade for truly scary kids TV. And as a kid in the Seventies who loved to be scared, it was wonderful.

Yes, I was that kind of child. I was a geek before it was cool to be a geek. I was brought up reading comic books. I used to win prizes for my model making, especially the Aurora glow-in-the-dark monster ones. I had a working scale model guillotine in my bedroom. I'd read *The Hunchback of Notre*

Dame and *War of the Worlds* in junior school. I'd done all this.

But I'd never seen a horror film. And that, I knew, was something I had to remedy.

The Exorcist was big news then and all the kids in my class at school claimed they had seen it. I never bothered to question how nine and ten year olds could be allowed into an X and I, who was big for my age, couldn't, but I believed them. And I felt left out. I had to do something about it. And there, in the *Radio Times* for that Friday night, was it. *Dracula Has Risen From the Grave.* I told my mother I was going to stay up to watch it. She, surprisingly, I thought, said fine. So I did. And I still remember that experience vividly.

The credits crashed in. Discordant, ominous music. 'Dracula' writ large on the screen. Ten-year-old me shuddered. Then the credits finished and . . . some kid on a bike. He looks happy. He's whistling. What, I thought? Was this a Hammer film? Was this scary? No. I can take this. The kid on the bike goes to the local church, throws his bike down on the steps in a manner I was always being told off for doing, goes inside. Takes a broom, starts to sweep up. A little too enthusiastically, I thought.

Then goes to ring the bell. He pulls the rope. It won't ring. He looks at his hands. Red. Blood red. He screams.

I was starting to get scared.

The priest hurries into the church. The bike is missing from the steps now. I knew he should have locked it. He goes up the steps to the bell tower. Finds a trail of blood.

By now, ten-year-old me is having palpitations.

The priest follows the blood to the bell where . . . a dead girl, blood running from the twin wounds in her neck, falls out.

And that was enough for me. Off to bed I went.

And yet . . . and yet . . .

I wasn't going to give up. I vowed that wouldn't be the end. Oh no. I wasn't going to be beaten. So I tried again. An old Universal black and white one this time. *Frankenstein*, all English camp staginess and German Expressionism. Dead easy. No trouble. And they were great, but they weren't Hammer. So, emboldened, I tried again. Karloff and Lugosi were my gateway drug. Lee and Cushing were the hard stuff. And that was it. I was hooked.

After that, Hammer films (and Amicus and Tigon, even) took up a huge part of my childhood.

I bought, and still have, every issue of *The House of Hammer* magazine (or whatever it was calling itself that particular month), Alan Frank and Denis Gifford's big, lavishly illustrated books on horror films, and everything I could get my hands on. And when the BBC started its horror double bills on a Saturday night . . . I was in heaven. Or hell, whichever you prefer.

I can't tell you how much I loved these films. And still do. Their gloriously Technicolor, gory, gothic sensibilities are now hard-wired into my writing DNA. I've got an embarrassingly large collection of Hammer DVDs and Blu-Rays. And I still watch them. All the way through, this time.

So when I got a call asking me to write the sequel to *The Woman In Black* for Hammer Books I jumped at it. Didn't hesitate, didn't stop to think. My name and Hammer on the spine of a book? No brainer.

But then . . . Hold on. I'd just agreed to write the sequel to one of the greatest ghost stories of all time. Could I do it? I don't know. The only thing I did know was that if I didn't do it, they would ask someone else. And that would be worse than not doing it at all.

And the other thing that attracted me was it wasn't just an exercise in nostalgia. I didn't want to do a retread of the original novel any more than Hammer wants to make films that would only appeal to an audience from fifty years ago. Hammer are unapologetically making the kind of films you would hope the original crew would be making if they had continued into the twenty-first century.

So I've given it my best shot. I hope I've not only honoured the original novel but also written something that would thrill that ten-year-old boy who was too terrified to look but desperately wanted to keep watching. This is for him. And that whole generation of movie watchers and book readers who grew up alongside him. But it's also for the next generation who are watching all-new Hammer films through their fingers and learning just how great it is to be scared.

Martyn Waites
July 2013

About Hammer

Hammer is the most well-known film brand in the UK, having made over 150 feature films which have been terrifying and thrilling audiences worldwide for generations.

Whilst synonymous with horror and the genre-defining classics it produced in the 1950s to 1970s, Hammer was recently rebooted in the film world as the home of "Smart Horror", with the critically acclaimed *Let Me In* and *The Woman in Black*. With *The Woman in Black: Angel of Death* scheduled for 2014, Hammer has been re-born.

Hammer's literary legacy is also now being revived through its new partnership with Arrow Books. This series features original novellas by some of today's most celebrated authors, as well as classic stories from nearly a century of production.

In 2014 Hammer Arrow will publish books by DBC Pierre, Lynne Truss and Joanna Briscoe as well as a novelisation of the forthcoming *The Woman in Black: Angel of Death*, continuing a programme that began with bestselling novellas from Helen Dunmore and Jeanette Winterson. Beautifully produced and written to read in a single sitting, Hammer Arrow books are perfect for readers of quality contemporary fiction.

For more information on Hammer
visit: www.hammerfilms.com or
www.facebook.com/hammerfilms

The Woman in Black
Susan Hill

'Heartstoppingly chilling'
Daily Express

Arthur Kipps, a junior solicitor, is summoned to attend the funeral of
Mrs Alice Drablow, the sole inhabitant of Eel Marsh House, unaware
of the tragic secrets which lie hidden behind the shuttered windows.

The house stands at the end of a causeway, wreathed in fog and
mystery, but it is not until Arthur glimpses a wasted young woman,
dressed all in black, at the funeral, that a creeping sense of unease
begins to take hold, a feeling deepened by the reluctance of the
locals to talk of the woman in black – and her terrible purpose.

'A rattling good yarn, the sort that chills the mind
as well as the spine'
Guardian

'An excellent ghost story...magnificently eerie...
compulsive reading'
Evening Standard

VINTAGE BOOKS
London